The author, Alan Charles Harrison, has written six books over a three-year period from the age of seventy to eighty years. He has been an artist and musician all his life. Family life and his children were at the heart of his hobbies.

Beginning an apprenticeship at British Rail and working as a craftsman over forty years was foremost in bringing up his family. His artistic life and musical career spans over sixty years. Even at present age of eighty-one, he is still active with a singing partner as a duo entertaining. He had a dormant period when his wife died on his seventieth birthday. This went on for five years. His singing partner eventually lit the spark that invigorated his musical and artistic life. It was during this period from his seventy-seventh year to his eightieth that his paint brush changed to the pen, finding a way to forward his creation so he turned to Austin Macauley.

I would like to give my sincere thanks to my granddaughter, Hayley Louise Harrison, for typing the text from my longhand writing. Without her constant encouragement, I would never have brought this book to a conclusion.

Alan Charles Harrison

IVANHOE MILL

AUSTIN MACAULEY PUBLISHERS™
LONDON • CAMBRIDGE • NEW YORK • SHARJAH

Copyright © Alan Charles Harrison (2020)

The right of Alan Charles Harrison to be identified as author of this work has been asserted by the author in accordance with section 77 and 78 of the Copyright, Designs and Patents Act 1988.

All rights reserved. No part of this publication may be reproduced, stored in a retrieval system, or transmitted in any form or by any means, electronic, mechanical, photocopying, recording, or otherwise, without the prior permission of the publishers.

Any person who commits any unauthorised act in relation to this publication may be liable to criminal prosecution and civil claims for damages.

This is a work of fiction. Names, characters, businesses, places, events, locales, and incidents are either the products of the author's imagination or used in a fictitious manner. Any resemblance to actual persons, living or dead, or actual events is purely coincidental.

A CIP catalogue record for this title is available from the British Library.

ISBN 9781528975063 (Paperback)
ISBN 9781528975087 (ePub e-book)

www.austinmacauley.com

First Published (2020)
Austin Macauley Publishers Ltd
25 Canada Square
Canary Wharf
London
E14 5LQ

To my dear friend, Brenda Thread Gold, for the constant encouragement as my writings progressed.

Table of Contents

Chapter One — 11
Cawston Manor

Chapter Two — 17
The Forge

Chapter Three — 24
The Acorn Inn

Chapter Four — 34
Joe Grommit

Chapter Five — 42
The Market

Chapter Six — 45
The Storm

Chapter Seven — 52
The Boat Trip

Chapter Eight — 73
Discussions at Cawston Manor

Chapter Nine — 84
The Boisterous Acorn Inn

Chapter Ten — 91
Friends on the River

Chapter Eleven — 115
Katie Returns to Cawston Manor

Chapter One
Cawston Manor

A fresh covering of snow emptied its contents from the early morning sky, giving the landscape a look of beauty. James Sanderson walked through the virgin snow. His boots imprinting a track between two parallel rows of beech trees which led to the big house at the top of the hill on the estate of Cawston Manor.

The beech trees were accepting the falling snow on their overhanging branches, which formed a tangled framework of eeriness. Their shapes made him shudder a little inside as he imagined the mass of branches to be a giant black spider's web that would drop down on him. His young body would be devoured by eight legged monsters that hung above. The snow-covered impregnated network above him had fired his imagination. He scolded himself for letting his train of thought disturb his mind. He must preserve himself for the task he had been sent to do by his father Rusty Sanderson, the village blacksmith at Ivanhoe Forge.

James was being made responsible for a task of work he had been sent to do at Cawston Manor. Feeling rather nervous as he made his way to the big house, he stopped beside the large black trunk of a beech tree. Placing his bag of tools on the snow-covered ground, he rubbed his frozen hands feverishly. Stamping his feet with vigour, trying to get some life into his frozen extremities, he unbuttoned his breeches with difficulty and relieved himself at the side of the big tree.

He watched with relief as the riverlet of steaming urine threaded its way down the rough bark and formed a steamy pool at the feet of James.

James arranged his clothing appropriately picking up his heavy bag and slinging it deftly over his shoulder. He walked up the hill towards the big house. James reached the end of the parallel row of trees and walked a short way to the side entrance of Cawston Manor. James looked nervously at the large heavily panelled door, a fine iron knocker, and solidly fastened to the door was the tool James had to use to indicate his presence and purpose of his visit.

James slung his heavy bag from his shoulder and sighed with relief as he placed it on the snow-covered porch. He looked at the large door knocker which seemed to be telling him to do the job it was there for. He chastised himself for feeling so inadequate. "Pull yourself together," he said to himself under his breath, "You are nowt but a wimp, show some spunk you've been sent to do a job of work, there's nowt can harm thee, your dad would be having a rate laugh if he could see you quivering like a jelly, go on get on with it, there's nowt to be fabled about."

James plucked up courage to use the knocker, "I will knock hard, I will show you, you're only a big lump of iron, I will be your master." James reached out with his cold frosted hand and held the equally cold lump of iron in his grasp. "I will thump this big door; I will show you that I am your master!" Two solid knocks were struck on the large panelled door. "There, I've struck the first blow!" James took a step back, making a space between him and the door. He now waited nervously for an occupant inside the manor to open the door. He would state his presence and hope that he will be accepted with kindness.

Rusty, James' father, had primed James with a few handling tips to cope with any awkwardness that was levelled at him. "Just let your words speak your way, keep thee head, do as tha's told to suit their orders and that'll be alreet." After another knock, James did three bangs after a feeling of being ignored. He started getting a bit uppity with himself. "I have not come all this way like a looney to be left like a beggar, I have come to do a job of work," he said under his breath.

James was now getting agitated; he was about to have another go at the lump of iron in front of him when the door slowly creaked open. His heart started to pound. The door opened just enough to expose the shape of a large figure looking sternly at him from the confines of the entrance of the manor. The door opened more, fully exposing a most fearsome, robust and large woman. Her rounded face and small penetrating eyes looked sternly at the nervous young man on the wet porch. "What's your business at this early hour?" The aggressive, frightening figure barked in a nasty manner at James.

The door was now fully open, her large figure filled the door entrance. Her scowling attitude to James had taken him aback. He had now passed the shock of this unpleasant bully who stood before him. He wanted now to retaliate and compete with her aggression. Thinking what his father had warned him about, he tempered his thoughts down to a submissive level of confrontation.

"Well?" The big woman snarled, "State your presence or be off with you." She stood facing James, her large, fat arms folded across her chest supporting the heaviness of her breasts.

"I excuse any inconvenience I have caused, Ma'am. I have been sent by my father, Rusty Sanderson, to do a job of work at the Manor. I am at your service if you please."

The big lady dropped her arms from across her chest and said, "Wait here," and closed the door on James.

He waited for his acceptance to do his job of work. After what seemed forever, the woman was back. The big door was swiftly opened and the now agitated James was ordered into the manor.

James picked up his bag of tools and went through the opened door.

"Hat off young man," she scowled again with aggression. She looked at poor James as he took off his sodden hat as instructed.

"I am James Sanderson; Ma'am I am here at the command of Mr Cawston to do certain duties. This paper tells you what I am here to do." James offered the grubby note to the woman. "Don't bother me with bits of paper!" she snapped. "It's out of my business, I have more important tasks to keep me occupied, follow me and be sharp about it."

James followed the large woman as she went down the dull, dimly lit corridor. The big woman stopped at a large panelled door. She knocked sharply, cocked her head, listening for the command from within. James was standing behind the big woman, his bag of tools weighing heavily on his shoulder. A reply came from the room beyond the closed door, "Enter!" a broad sounding command was heard, the large brass door knob was turned by the woman and the door was pushed open exposing a luxurious layout of splendour. "This is James Sanderson, sire. I leave him in your care, sire. I have much work to do, if you require anything further for me to do, I am at your disposal."

She spoke with an air of importance but the Lord of the Manor was not impressed by her sarcastic attitude. He tolerated her only for her usefulness at keeping check on his staff. He needed her powers of observation to keep him informed of discrepancies and misdeeds that may occur in the manor. "That will be all, Emily," she turned smartly with a nod of her head and with an icy look at James, closed the door behind her.

James felt quite alone and nervous at being face to face with the Lord of the Manor. "Relax young man, you have nothing to fear from me, I have been informed by your father of your increasing skills. Rusty has done many favourable jobs for me over the years, you as his apprentice and son, I am sure you have picked up the skills your father has taught you. I am confident you are the man for the job."

"Thank you, sir, I am at your service," said James. "I am Gunston Cawston and you, young James, are a valuable asset to me, with the skills you and your father offer. I want you to completely relax and I will give you all of the details of the job in hand. When the deed is finished to my satisfaction, you will be rewarded accordingly. Before you leave, you will go to my kitchen and fill with a belly of good food."

"I thank you kindly, Sir. I will gladly serve you and hope my work is to your pleasure." James felt at ease with Gunston Cawston, the aggression of Emily the house maid was surely more difficult compared with the Master. His comfort inside the manor gladdened his heart. He felt that with the Master on his side, he could stand up to the nastiness of Emily to his advantage. "Pardon me one moment, young James. I must write a note of instruction to your father, I have a number of things to clarify."

James stood stiffly to attention as the Master put his pen to paper. Gunston Cawston's lean figure was smartly dressed, the rich coloured sepia waistcoat he wore fitted smartly to his lithe body. His matching garments added to the correctness of his attire.

James looked around the room as the Master of Cawston Manor was putting pen to paper. The large, highly polished desks cluttered with papers and books was looked upon by James as his first experience of such an unusual sight.

The large semi-circular bay window with deep red burgundy draped curtains amplified the morning light. Snow was steadily falling as James looked through the large window. The richly decorated room was filled with beautiful elegant furniture. Heavy shelves all around the room housed rows of books, pictures and silverware, multi-coloured trinkets, and things James had never seen before. The room he stood in, facing the Master of Cawston, was so magical it took his breath away.

Gunston Cawston had finished his instructions on paper for Rusty Sanderson. He looked kindly at James, folded the note, putting it into an envelope. James stepped forward to the edge of the large desk and took the message from the master for his father. "Now then, young James, we will now get on with the task you have come here to perform. I will give you the assistance of one of my servants to help with your project, then you will be left to your own devices to complete the work. Be off with you now, young man, if there are any problems, tell your assistant and it will be done. Oh, and by the way, a good feed in the kitchen will be available. Tell your father, I will shortly be in touch, that's all." James nodded respectfully and closed the heavy door behind him.

Chapter Two
The Forge

The forge at Ivanhoe Mill was active as Rusty Sanderson and his son James were making an early start with their work load of orders from Cawston Manor. James had been to the big house the day before but he had difficulty completing the job of work that had been allotted to him by Rusty. He had a rough time and struggled with certain aspects of his task. He had done most of the work to the best of his ability but needed more work to be done at the forge. The snow had fallen more heavily overnight. The strong wind had caused drifts of unmanageable proportions.

Rusty and James had to dig their way into the forge to open the entrance door. It was so early in the morning to be held back by the atrocious weather. The day had started badly before they had gotten to the forge. "Get thi sen moving lad, let's have some life int fire we've been held back with that white stuff outside, let's get some heat int the place." James primed the coals trying to ignite the stubborn match wood. The fire was not playing the game this morning. After much perseverance the flame took hold of the coals.

"There Father, there's nowt to it," said James grinning at his dad with pride. "Tha took thee time, it'll be snap time before we get started, and half of day's gone already! Get thee finger out and mash a can of sweet tea, it'll get us moving a bit."

"Giv us a bit longer Dad, a bit more life's needed int fire." James pumped furiously with the crude set of bellows transforming the fire flames into a white heat. Bright sparks flew up into the chimney, to exit out of sight to the coldness of the early morning.

"I'll get tha tea now pa," said James. "Fire's going a treat now, place is warming up, it's good to be inside leaving the cold out th-ya."

"Get on with it then lad," chirped Rusty. "Flame'll be dead again if thy loiters. We've got some brass to get together, we can't mess about all day, come on or I'll scuff thee." James proceeded with his domestic task in silence pulling comical faces behind Rusty's back. "Where's the billy can, dad?" said James. "Use thee eyes lad, it'll not come runnin' up to thee." James pulled another cheeky face at Rusty.

The can was amongst the clutter, James flicked the billy can from the bench at the side of the now white, hot fire that Rusty was bellowing. He deftly caught it by its wire handle before it hit the floor. "Tha'll miss t-andle one of these days and come unstuck with thee trickery, let's see how good thee are at brewing, there's a ton of graft waiting when thee's finished larking, get on we it!"

James left the warmth of the forge squeezing through the gap in the partly open door. The thick drifted snow outside wedged it to the limit of its opening. James filled the billy can with snow and hastily closed the door, keeping out the rawness outside. "Things look quiet over yon Dad, no sign or movement about." Rusty looked at James, he was still activating the bellows, "The'll not see much of that lot at this hour, the ale that's guzzled over the're does the job of keeping 'em quiet to much later than us. Idol sots! Don't know what it is to graft, note but wasters that's what they are."

The ale house, set well back from the forge, was the local den of iniquity. The sordid activity, the scheming and misdemeanour was a magnet for many unscrupulous dealings that were borne there. "We don't want to be tagged wi there sort lad! Remain true to the feelings of the heart, a good clean living is a more honest answer to the likes of that lot, we can sleep calm in our bed knowing that the brass we mek with hard graft, keeps the honest coppers rolling in." James handed Rusty hot steaming tea, the fire white hot comforting them. "About time yer young wimp!" said Rusty. He winked at James; the pride of his life was atonic. They worked so well together, making the hard work they performed most pleasurable. They were at one with the world, a good seem to be in.

"I suppose thy wants somet in thee belly now?" said Rusty to his expectant son. "If thy's got owt Dad, it would be a good start to get me movin' wi me tools."

"Pass us me package over there," said Rusty, "See what we've got, I suppose thee belly's grumbling as it always is?" Holding the tin of hot brew, James looked expectantly at his father as he unwrapped the package. A large piece of bread filled with a thick lump of cheese was today's belly filler. Rusty broke the food in two halves, James looked at the two unequal halves and went for the biggest.

Rusty had his thumb on that one. "Tha's done it again Dad, you always hold thee thumb ant biggest, it's my turn today, all the graft I did at the big house for you yesterday, I thought you'd gimme a treat today." Rusty looked at James, a mischievous look in his eyes. "You had your belly filled with all them goodies at the big house, that shudda filled thee belly for a week! The lovely Emily musta smothered ya wi all that tuck." James replied, "Her beady eyes were on me all the time, she made me feel guilty at every mouthful, 've got to tangle with her again when I go back to the big house, can't you go Dad? She gives me the scary's." James' father looked at him and replied, "Don't be a ninny, a young 18-year-old strapping lad like thee shunt be fazed by an old biddy! Use thee ed and get round 'er with a bit of the old charm, tha's got to start somewhere lad!"

James chuckled, "I'm not starting wi her dad, I want a lass young and fresh!"

Rusty looked at his handsome son, "There's time for that game when thy's finished thee training, that's enough idle chat, finish thee snap, lets gerund with some graft." Business now returned to the forge.

Rusty and James were consumed by their daily work load. It had started snowing at a heavier rate. The wind was howling, and Rusty had thoughts of staying at the forge tonight. The severe cold would be hard to bear in their shack which was only a short distance from the forge. The comforts around the fire will be more bearable than the coldness of their shack. "That's is," said Rusty. "We stay 'ere tonight."

The industrious activity inside the forge was disrupted by a knocking on the door outside. "Listen lad," said Rusty, "It's there again." James went to the door; it was jammed shut. A hard push opened it further, James saw a hand through the gap in the door. "Dad, quick, there's someone out 'ere laid out!" Rusty went over to James and saw the hand through the gap. They pushed the door open enough for James to squeeze through. "It's a woman!" shouted James. Rusty instructed, "Push her away from the door," and joined his son. They lifted the woman into the forge laying her gently beside the warmth of the fire.

"It's Tilly Blagdon, Sam Lister's woman, she's wet and frozen, hardly breathing! Wonder why she's here?" questioned James looking at Rusty.

"There must be somet wrong at their place, what shall we do, Dad?" Rusty replied. "Tha's got to go ova to the Acorn Inn." He looked at James, "Ask Charlie Horner to send Rosie o-a, say that we want her here quick, fetch plenty of warm coverings, be sharpish lad, this is a bad job!"

James prepared himself to face the fierce elements outside. "Be as quick as thee can lad," said James as he left the comfort of the Forge. The sharp wind was strong and cruel driving the falling snow into deep drifts. James fought his way through the storm toward the Acorn Inn, silhouetted in the distance. James reached the inn; his desperate struggle had exhausted him. He knocked on the heavy door, shouting as loud as he could above the howling wind. Eventually, his presence was heard from within. The door opened a little, the gruff voice of Charlie Horner scowled at the distressed young James, "What's all the banging about, lad, at this early hour?"

James replied, "I need help, you must send help to the forge Mr Horner." James told the landlord the problem.

His attitude to James became more compassionate, "We need Rosie. Dad said, ask Rosie, there's no time to waste, Tilly Blagden's in a bad way." Charlie replied, "I'll sort Rosie out." James stood anxiously waiting for Charlie Horner to raise Rosie from her quarters. She soon appeared carrying some warm coverings. "Come on young James, let's be off." They both struggled back to the forge. "Open up Dad," shouted James as they neared the forge door, "Open up."

Rusty heard the shouts from within. The door opened, the two exhausted figures of James and Rosie were thanked by Rusty for their speedy return. Rusty looked at Rosie as she knelt down at the stricken Tilly. She said, "I think she's gone; I fear there's somet wrong at their place." Rosie was thinking about the two girls and said, "Well where is Sam Lister?" Rusty said, "I am going over to their place, if there's somet wrong with Sam the two young lasses will be on their own, I'm going ova now."

Rusty prepared himself for the trip to Sam Lister's farm. "You two stay 'ere, I will be soon back." Rusty was off to find the solution to this sad incident.

The bad weather had no let up. Rusty fought gallantly through the deep snow. He reached Lister's place, shouting Sam's name. "Sam, can thee hear me lad? Mek a call Sam, mek a call." Nothing but silence. The door to the cottage was ajar, Rusty went in. "Call if tha's in Sam, I've come to see if thy's alreet." There was silence. Rusty went further into the room looking for any signs of life. He heard a whimper in the corner of the room. "Hello, who's there?" Rusty went to the place he heard the sound coming from.

A pile of hessian coverings was piled in the corner. Rusty parted them and revealed the two lasses huddled together. Tilly Blagdon's kids looked near to their end. Rusty gathered them up and cuddled them up to the inside of his thick coat. He made his way back to the forge. The two frozen lasses hugged to his chest. He traced his own tracks back to the forge hoping desperately that he could keep life into the youngens. On his way back he saw James coming toward him. "What's happened Dad?" Rusty handed one of the young lasses to James. "Wrap her in your coat lad, we must get back quickly or we'll lose these two." They reached the forge; Rosie heard their shouts. She opened the door.

Shock was showing on Rosie's pale face. James and Rusty put the two lasses on the warm coverings beside the warmth of the forge fire. They desperately rubbed the frozen limbs of the two girls trying to spark life into their young bodies. The older child looked more hopeful than the other. She was responding in a fair way. Rosie looked at the two men looking down on her. "I think the youngens gone," she said. Tears ran down her pale face and her sobs started. Her mother Tilly Blagdon was covered on the floor. Rosie laid her small lassie beside her and she broke down uncontrollably, and went to the open arms of Rusty.

Rusty held Rosie, his comfort was her need. James sadly looked on, this was the saddest and most traumatic day of his young life. As the day progressed, words soon spread of the tragedy that had happened to Tilly Blagdon and her kids. The talking point that people were asking was where was Sam Lister? He had not been seen since the night before. Charlie Horner had seen him early doors the previous day. He had called at the Acorn Inn to see one of his lads. It was noted by Charlie but he didn't stay for long.

Tilly Blagdon and her youngen were to be picked up from the forge by the undertaker. The elder Blagdon lassie was recovering and being looked after by Rusty and James. That was the only pleasing thing that had happened on this most awful day. The weather was too severe for the removal of Tilly and her lassie. Rosie had volunteered to stay with Rusty and James, supporting them with the trauma in the forge. Charlie Horner had sent some food and necessities to them from The Acorn. Plenty of compassion and help was offered by the surrounding neighbours. In the next few days, the tragedy was under control. The weather had subsided and the relief was blessed.

The mystery was still the disappearance of Sam Lister. Over the next few days, the bad weather had subsided. The relief was enough for life to get more comfortable. The undertaker had done his job at the forge, and Rosie had taken young Poppy Blagdon back to the Acorn Inn to care for her.

The sadness of the tragedy had affected the villagers who knew the Blagdon's. Their compassion was a comfort to the sad, cruel incident. There was still the mystery of Sam Lister, the area had been scoured in many places. The river that ran at the back of the Acorn had been looked at for any sign of the tragedy. Nothing could be found of Sam, and his disappearance had made things very serious.

Many friends of Sam looked for a conclusion to his disappearance.

Chapter Three
The Acorn Inn

Charlie Horner was at his wit's end; he was enveloped in the unruliness at the Ivanhoe Inn. Fighting and bickering went on with the out of control crowd. Charlie looked at the drunken man lying on the Inn floor. "Throw him out," said Charlie looking at his two trusted friends. "The sort is note but a loada rabble, I can't afford his sort clogging up the floor." Charlie helped his two friends to carry the unwanted problem from the room, dumping him outside in the cold night.

"I have got to sort this mess out," said Charlie to his two friends, "I'm ready to crack up." Charlie looked ill at ease, "I'm ready to do a runner, I've lost it, there's no pleasure in the game now, somets gotta be put rate or I go under." He looked at the signs of support from his friends who replied, "Come on Charlie, things'll look better when thy's had some kip, thy's got lots going for thee, sort thee sen out when thy's feeling more uppity."

"Thanks for the support," Charlie replied, "I'll get through the rubbish, the light might shine brighter when I've pulled mesen together." His friend replied, "Tha's a gooden for us Charlie, the lad'll not let thee fall, come on, get thee sen inside, lets gerr among that lot, we are with thee, tek rough wit smooth and job'll be a gooden."

Mayhem still dominated the crowded room; Charlie's frustrations had subsided. He went back into the cauldron of discontent and went through the motions of being the landlord.

A man's heavy booted foot kicked the dog that lay beside the warm smouldering fire. Its teeth bared and changed the placidness of the animal to its instincts of survival. "You bullying sot," the dog's owner stood up sharply. His chair falling backwards with the speed of his angry reaction. "Lift a boot to my dog, you bloody scoundrel." The dog's master grabbed the offender gripping the cloth on the upper part of his coat. His big callused hands screwing it tight around his neck, putting his tough looking face up to the offending man. He screwed the clothing tighter around the man's throat. The toughness of his grip making the man's eyes bulge and his face red with fear.

"Apologise to my dog, you unsavoury sot, or I will not let go of your scrawny neck! What does tha feel like being sorted out in this way? Thy's more to come to thee if the rate words don't come out of thee ugly gob, come on what's it to be? As thee lost the voice, tha jabbering loada crap!"

He stuttered through his clenched black unsightly teeth, his slaver dripping through his scruffy beard. "I will, I will."

"Come on then, let's hear it, se thee piece or I'll not let go of thee" Josh Tetley got the words he wanted and let go of the tightness around the man's throat. "On thee way now, hop it, I'll be watching thee, tharl be on my list to sort out if thee crosses me again." The inn had been silenced by the actions of Josh Tetley; the rowdiness soon returned as the incident reached its conclusion.

Josh Tetley drew a rough gnarled pipe from his waistcoat pocket. He slowly tapped the spent tobacco from its bowl and refilled it from its pouch on the rough wooden table. A lit taper from the fire was placed in the freshly filled bowl and the flame was pulled with deep breaths igniting new life into his pipe. The expelled smoke rose into the air strengthening the thick cloud above. "Not now, Rosie." Josh cold shouldered the pestering pub favourite who gave her pleasured favours to her most desirable customers.

Rosie sat beside Josh, placing her chubby hand on his thigh. "Scram Rosie, I've business in hand, maybe later." Josh jerked his head at the rejected Rosie, the motion was enough for her to heed his signal for dismissal. Josh and his friends at the table were watching the door entrance waiting for the arrival of their associates. Two strangers entered the Inn, their contacts had arrived. They pushed their way through the crowded room to Josh Tetley's table and greeted the occupants with slight acknowledgement.

Josh caught the attention of a serving wench and signalled two ales for the table. Josh placed a coin into her hand, squeezed her rounded buttocks and winked his approval at the cheeky way she acknowledged his flirtiness. "Well gentlemen," said Josh, "Let's talk!" Josh sucked pleasurably at his pipe, it was threaded through his fat, strong fingers of one hand, and holding his pewter mug in the other, raised it to all around the table. "To our success, may the cards be in our favour." There was agreement all round.

Josh looked intently at the two men who had joined them. Jason Lines and Dan Liversidge were high up in the hierarchy of the crime scene around the Great Dearne Valley waterway network.

"The deal is fixed!" Jason Lines spoke, "Be ready in a few days, I'll make the usual contact, just be there for the pickup. We drink to that." Josh looked at his two partners, they lifted their vessels in approval to the deal. "We've come a long way to be here tonight Josh, Dan and I would like to be rewarded with your hospitality."

"I've arranged that pleasure, Dan and yourself have been afforded the perfect reward! You have two rooms booked to suit your pleasures." Josh winked at Jason and Dan. Their acknowledged approval was there to be taken at their own convenience. "Two sweet lassies will be available for the night; the entertainment is guaranteed." Jason Lines discreetly placed a guinea in the palm of Josh's hand. "You're in the gold league tonight, my friend, it's a step up from your silver dealing, keep dishing out your copper to the foot soldiers and your rewards will become the colour of the guinea in your palm."

Josh looked at Jason and then Liversidge with an interested sparkle in his eye. "The colour in my hand excites me," said Josh, "Working with you is fine by me." Jason and Dan were ready to retire, Josh told his friends to be discreet when they retired to the rooms above the inn. "The stairs over yon," said Josh, "Second door left, two sharp knocks. Dan is next door." Jason Lines and Dan Liversidge had now departed from their company. "I think we are on a winner!" said Josh. His two friends were pleased with the promise.

The mood in the large smoky room had now filled with the sound of music. Pepie, the self-appointed village minstrel was surrounded by a noisy, singing and boisterous crowd. He played his fiddle with gusto, the mellow tones of his instrument pleasured all around him. As the night came to a gradual end, Charlie Horner, the landlord was thinning his custom out into the night air. He was ready to call time. The Inn had served its usefulness for another day.

As the weeks passed by, the harsh winter had now mellowed into a more comfortable period. The earlier tragedy of the Blagdon's was fading away, there was still many questions unanswered.

Poppy, the elder daughter of Tilly Blagdon, was now being looked after by Rosie at the acorn inn. Information gleaned from young Poppy; she had shed no light into what happened on the sad day of the tragedy. There was still no sign of Sam Lister, it was a mystery to many people's mind, his two brothers were now active in keeping the farm in order. Tilly Blagdon and her youngest child were laid to rest. Rusty Sanderson and his fine, young son James were now back in their settled routine in the forge. Their work load was increasing. The improving weather contributed to a more active Forge.

"I suppose they'll be sending me to the big house we some of this lot?" James looked at Rusty, "Weather's in our favour now, lad, the sooner we get it sorted we get the brass for our effort." James looked at Rusty, "Can I talk to thee without thee getting uppity?" said James. "I am all ears lad, say it how you are thinking, I won't bite thee!" James looked at his father, searching for a way to say what troubled him. "It's like this Dad, I went up to the big house a week or so gone to take a few bits and pieces for the ongoing job as we were doing. Emily, the sour faced house keeper, was more like, well she happened to be more liking to me, she wasn't scowling and eyeballing with her little beady eyes, the feeds she offered were more giving."

Rusty smirked with mischief, looked at James, his jocular reply not taken kindly. He knew Rusty was joking, "Append she fancies thee young body, James lad. A young buck like thee may have turned her tap on."

"Give ova father, you're turning my asking for your advice silly," replied James. He looked in a more serious way at Rusty, "What I'm trying to say is my eye has been taken by a smart lassie at the manor. I had a good feeling towards her, I know she was looking at me with the same thoughts as I had. She is new at the manor and it's a thought in me as how getting to know her in a friendly way, I don't want to be fooled into embarrassment, what should I do Father?"

Rusty looked at James in a more serious way, his thoughts of how to guide James and sort his thoughts out were straight forward to him. He could only advise the lad as to how he would deal with it. James may have his own idea of his thoughts. "This young lassie," said Rusty, "Where does she come from?"

"She lives at lime crags across the bridge, her dad is church vicar, she's working at the big house as from a while back." Rusty looked at James with a weary look on his face,

"Thy has to be canny about her, don't get tangled with the lassie till tha's checked what she's about, thee dunt want to get burnt, if thy's not sure about her, play it cool lad. There's note wrong we having feelings for someone bonny that makes thee feel good, do as the sense tells thee and thy'll be alreet."

James quietly carried on with the work, he could analyse Rusty's advice at his leisure.

The harsh winter was being replaced by the welcome spring. Rusty Sanderson and son James were in a more settled state. The nightmare of the winter tragedy now passed. The memories were still coming back from time to time. James looked at his father Rusty, he had things on his mind that needed answers. "Dad," said Rusty, "That explosion at lime crags, a time back two years or so ago, does tha know the tale of it?" Rusty looked at his son with interest. "I know the tale that was said at the time, but there were different tales of blame, I know that three lads were killed with a fall of rock and Joe Grommit, a long-time friend of mine, was badly disabled and disfigured in his face. He was blamed, but they settled the tragedy as an accident, they set Joe Grommit up at the crags as a form of compensation looking after the site. He lives in a shack in the confines of the quarry with his mongrel. I've not seen him for a long time but tales are that he's become a recluse, himself because of his terrible disfigurement. His brother keeps an eye on his welfare but Joe wants the seclusion to do his own thing."

"Why I'm asking," said James, "Is that the lassie, I'm sweet on, talked of the happenings of the tragedy, her father the vicar did the church servicing. Rusty looked at his son, "As I said to thee before, play it cool with the lassie, don't be rushed into any problems, and you should come out with a fair piece of mind." James looked at Rusty, he still wanted a few things cleared up that bothered him. "You would never say ought about Ma," said James. Rusty looked at his son, he was taken aback by the words from James.

Rusty's silence towards his son was prolonged, he answered sharply in anger, "Tha's asking what I'd like kept under wraps James," in a choked manner. "When the time is right, I will open up to thee and it will be to thy advantage."

Rusty pulled a white-hot iron from the fire, "Let's get on with making today's brass, the talking for now is done." Rusty looked at his puzzled son and he quietly settled doing the job in hand leaving the question unanswered.

Spring was in the air, the young handsome James Sanderson left the forge and set off to Cawston Manor. Rusty had given his son some free time to pleasure himself with and free him from the daily hard toil at the forge. James had hopes of connecting with the young lassie from Lime Craggs who was a new housemaid at the big house. His heart was stirred with the hope of binding their friendship, his mindful intentions had put him in a mood of extreme pleasure.

He was diverting the purpose of his visit to the big house as an excuse to check on the outstanding job that he and Rusty were involved with. It must be made to look at the house staff that the young lassie which James had his desires on was protected from any chance of inappropriateness that may put her position at Cawston in danger. He was conscious of any gossip. She was also under strict supervision of Emily who held a reign on the staff at the big house. James didn't want any friction from her, she had cooled her tyranny towards James. Since the tragedy of the past winter he felt more comfortable with her, more relaxed in his manner towards her.

James walked briskly through the large iron double gates towards the big house in the distance. The road to the manor was a gradual slope, the two fine parallel rows of large beech trees which led to the big house were now shown in a different light. James still had thoughts of the struggle when they were in the grip of the not long past winter. The cluttered thick branches which formed a connected tunnel when the heaviness of snow was settled on the branches above the beech trees were now gone.

James chuckled at the way his thoughts invented the myth of the large spiders that would consume him. He looked at the snow scene above which was now quite different. The black spiders were now growing a covering of bright new green that was a beautiful replacement for the creepiness of its winter coat.

The parallel lines of beeches ended a fair distance from the Manor, James walked across the open space to the side door. He hoped it would be answered with a reception of friendliness, and hope that the bonnie lassie he hoped to see may be the one he confronts. She would certainly flip the heart of young James and would be the bonus he hoped for. The knock was soon answered, his heart missed a beat. "James, what brings you here again on this fine day?" James looked at the figure before him, the fright of the earlier clashes with the bullish Emily were now more subdued.

"Emily, sorry to bother you!" James looked at the half smirking Emily, "It's just for a brief look at the ironwork in the parlour for me Father, if you please." Emily toned down to young James, she stood aside for James to enter the hallway, "Heard some good talk about you and Rusty sorting out that bad job with the Blagdon's and old Sam Lister still missing." She looked admiringly at James, "I had good brave thoughts of thee mentioned. I said to Mr Cawston he had a good sparkling opinion of your work in the manor."

James looked in a curious way at Emily, "What did he say to thee?" said James. "He kept walking around the room saying kind muttering like *well done, well done me boy*, his pleasing sayings were showing good thoughts from the master." James looked at Emily who had now warmed to him. "Before you go me lad nip to see me, some goodies will be wrapped for you and Rusty, give him the thumbs up for me."

Emily sent James to the parlour, "Look me up before you leave," her friendliness towards him was more comforting than their first confrontation. "Thank you, ma'am, I'll do my work and be on my way." James gave Emily a reassuring smile, she accepted with a friendly nod and left James alone in the parlour. He looked around the large room and went to the large open fire grate. His pretence of being there was the cover he was using to try and confront the lassie that took his desire.

After a while, and listening to any sign of noise from any servant that may be around the manor, James kept looking at the closed door in the parlour. His lassie may know that he was about, she knew he was due to visit this day. James hoped that a discreet enquiry from her would bring her to the room where James waited in anticipation.

After what seemed such an age of time, James thought that the chance of seeing the lassie would not happen. His thoughts were that Emily would soon do a check on him and that his planned visit to the big house was a waste of time.

There was a knock on the large parallel door, James opened the door in anticipation, the lassie and James faced each other, their shyness caused a silence from the confrontation. The lassie spoke first, her gentle voice spoke nervously, "I'm Katie. I know you're James Sanderson." A smile from Katie was the spark from James to acknowledge her introduction, "We have names now, Katie. I hope you would not be troubled at this way of meeting. I had to do it this way, to see you has been my desire."

Katie looked at the fine, handsome James, "My pleasure to meet like this is worth any chastisement that may come my way." James shook her tiny, delicate hand that was offered. James felt his desire for this fine young lassie increase to the most pleasurable feeling. Katie looked around nervously, "I have to go now James, if I am seen like this I will be chastised and in a bad light with Emily."

James looked admiringly at the lassie before him, "Thank you for making the effort to see me. You go now Katie; I would like to see you again." Katie looked at James, "That would give me much pleasure," she said, "We will find a better way than this." Katie backed from the room, touched the outstretched hand of James and with a friendly smile walked off out of sight.

Chapter Four
Joe Grommit

Joe Grommit hobbled laboriously in the woods around the confines of Lime Crags. He was checking his game traps set the day before. Casper, his scruffy brown mongrel, enjoyed the routines of their inspections of the game traps. "Here lad, to heel," Joe gave a brief order to Casper. "Here lad, stay!" Joe was leaning heavily on his stick that he used for supporting his disability. He saw a movement in the undergrowth. Casper bared his teeth, his growl sensing the disturbance in the bushes.

Joe hobbled closer, there was someone hiding in the thick bush. Joe laid his stick gently on the back of Casper. "Show thee face!" Joe snapped, "If tha's a mind to face me, let's be seeing you!" There was silence in the thick undergrowth, "I know tha's in there," Joe snapped. "Show thee sen now or me dog'll flush thee out." The movement in the bushed area was disturbed. "I come out, I come out to thee," a distressed figure faced the unsavoury looking Joe Grommit. Casper had his teeth bared; his presence answered by a low continuous growl. "Well if it ain't Chalky Bagshaw!" The tall slightly built figure, his covering garments grimy and ragged clung to the pathetic youth who stood before Joe.

"What's thee game?" snapped Joe Grommit, "You are the snivelling wretch that's been at my traps." Young Bagshaw had fear in his eyes, the threatening Joe could make times hard for Chalky if the word of Joe Grommit put a finger on him.

"Joe, I'm in bother, I have got hardship at home and I don't know how to get out from my plight." The pathetic figure before Joe looked at the end of his tether. Joe's own struggle in life was in a state of extreme hardship. His meagre existence was enhanced by his brave efforts of survival.

The sad Chalky Bagshaw was taken aback with the sight of the disfigured Joe Grommit. Before his accident, he was a respected and good-hearted chap to have in your corner. He had known young Chalky as a young cheeky sprog of a child. His fatherless family had struggled in a sorry state of poverty. Not much had gone their way over the years. Joe's compassionate side wanted to kick in and put the lad on a better path than his past.

"I'll offer thee some respite, young Chalky," said Joe, "Listen to what I've to say." Joe leaned heavily on his stick, "Settle Casper, settle old lad."

Chalky felt more at ease, Joe's facial disfigurement had shocked the lad. It was his first showing of him but his aggression had gone, and he was now offering the young Chalky a way out of his cheating on Joe Grommit's patch. "I know thy's been taking from me traps, when you take what's in 'em you set 'em in a way not as I have, that's why I know a snivelling rogue has snaffled from me, listen up young Chalky." Joe faced the young lad menacingly, he had been rumbled, the only way out was to listen to Joe Grommit.

Joe readjusted his stance as he faced the guilty young Chalky, "Listen to what I've to say lad, there's a way out for thee if thy's a mind to agree. I need a youngen to make things easier for me." Chalky took in the words that Joe Grommit put to him. "I can't get around much and do what I need to, tha can see my state, a youngen like thee could be what's needed and make things fair for the two of us." Young Chalky Bagshaw felt more at ease with words that Joe had put to him. "How does tha want me to help thee?" said Chalky. "Come back to my place youngen, tha'll see what I'm up against." The young Chalky agreed to Joe's words. He followed the crippled Joe Grommit and Casper through the woods back to Joe's shack.

They came to the ram shackle abode on the outer confines of the lime quarry. The quaint primitive building was roughly fenced around the shack. A pile of logs heaped around a rough sturdy bench in a cluttered space near the door entrance was the fuel stock for the fire. A small whisp of smoke rose from the chimney of the shack. "Fire inside needs feedin!" said Joe, "Grab a few bits from the pile young lad, lets' get some life back into the dying embers." Chalky heeded Joe's words and carried the logs inside. A small table and a sturdy wooden chair set back from the fire in the room centre was cluttered with vessels and articles of his domestic needs.

A bed in the corner with its ragged coverings was the comfort zone for Joe Grommit. A small window in the building was the only source of light, candles in various holders were placed around, and rough shelving in parts of the shack were crammed with Joe's needs. "Put them logs among the embers lad," said Joe, "Let's get some light into it."

Young Chalky did as was said, "That's it, lad," said Joe, "I feel more kindly toward thee Chalky lad. If thy can do as I need, the both of us can be as one." Joe looked at the young lad, "I feel it more comforting you being like you are to me Mr Grommit." Chalky looked at Joe with a gladness in his eye. "Call me Joe, you look after me as needs be and you'll be done well by me." The young Chalky Bagshaw had dropped into a good seam with Joe Grommit. After a fair amount of time the relationship moulded into an understanding that suited the pairs' needs. Joe's struggling with his disabling problems had subsided. Chalky had made a sound impact in the confines of Joe's residence. Wood chopping, taking charge of the game traps, fixing problems beyond Joe's capability, and generally making life much sweeter. The team work was a satisfactory spark that had blossomed in the humble confines of Lime Crags.

The young Chalky had made amiable contacts from some of Joe's work mates. They encouraged the way his friendship had developed into a most suitable conclusion. Chalky's struggling family had also benefited. Chalky's association with Joe Grommit had beneficial spin offs. There was fair contentment all around. In a relaxed moment, Joe Grommit and Chalky were seated around the warmth of the fire in the crude shack. The fire flames intermittently lit the room in a comforting way. Joe was puffing gently on his pipe, blowing uneven smoke rings, which rose slowly to the confines of the ceiling.

"Fancy a smoke, Chalky lad?" Joe looked at the silent Chalky who was staring with a blank expression into the fire. He looked at the scarred face of Joe, his disability gave Chalky no problem. He was now comfortable with the condition with Joe's disfigurement. "I'd like a puff, yes, I'd really like to smoke one of your pipes." Joe pointed to a crude wooden rack hanging on the wall beside the fire place. "Take hold of one of them lad." Chalky gently selected a pipe from the rack, "I know thy's not been smoking has the lad," said Joe looking enquiringly at him. "Not had the chance, if tha can show us the way I'll give it a go." Joe filled the chosen pipe with tobacco that Chalky had taken from its holder on the wall and gave it to the lad.

Chalky sucked at the flamed taper that Joe had lit from the fire, "Tha's into it now, lad," said Joe, "Keep pulling the air through, short quick breaths, that's it me lad, it's glowing like a beacon now."

Chalky started coughing and spluttering, "That's alreet. Take ya breath, keep tekin small puffs, the bowl will keep glowing if tha stops sucking it'll go out, a bit of practice'll do the job." Joe left the coughing and spluttering Chalky with the pipe and tendered the meal that cooked on the fire

The iron rig that held the cooking utensils was not to Joe's satisfaction. He had plans to update the rickety problem. "Dowse the pipe now lad, get thee sen over to sort this thing out." Chalky killed the life in the pipe, his smoking was put on hold.

"That seems to be at odds with the cooking Joe, that cradle holding the stew looks rough," said Chalky, "We'll fix it proper."

"I've got it sorted," said Joe, "Let's feed on our spoils and fill our chops with this tasty dish. If this dunt get thee taste buds pleasured, there's somet wrong with thee." Chalky licked his lips, giving Joe a smile of acceptance to the offer of the feed. "I'm having bother with the iron work set up that holds the cooking pans over the fire. It needs sorting, Chalky me lad." Chalky looked at Joe as he meddled awkwardly at the rough wire rig that held the utensils over the fire. "Does tha know young James Sanderson?" said Joe.

Chalky looked at Joe as he struggled around the fire with his flimsy iron supports. "I've grown up with him over the years since being a nipper," said the puzzled Chalky. "I've not been rate good chums with him, but he's fair and alreet, it feels as he's a lot more going for him than me. I think he's a smart kid." Joe eyed Chalky with thoughts of asking what he wanted to say. "Would thy be phased if I asked you to go to the forge at Ivanhoe mill to see the Sanderson's?" Chalky held back Joe's question, "For what purpose would you be sending me, Joe?" Joe left his pottering with the fire frame and sat at the table adjusting his chair to face the warm glowing fire.

Chalky sat opposite Joe and held his gaze, "Rusty Sanderson and I go back a long way, we had a good likeness for each other, he had his forge handed to him from family connections. He's had a good hold on it through his hard work, I don't see him at all now, but I do know he keeps enquiring a time or two of my keeping things how I've a mind to." Chalky listened to Joe's talking, "What's thee purpose of thee wanting to send me to see the Sanderson's?" Joe looked towards the fire, "The old iron works!" said Joe.

"I've heard it said that he'd give us the offer of sorting out the problem that I couldn't manage." Joe looked at Chalky pointing at the fire, he said "That's all I want Rusty to do and as things are now, I'm not proud to ask him."

"So that's it, Chalky lad, there's a trip to the forge for thee." Chalky got the answer that pleased him, "I go tomorrow," said Chalky. "Let's drink to that lad, put the can on for some tea!" replied Joe.

Chalky Bagshaw walked over the bridge that connected Lime Crags from Ivanhoe Mill. At Joe Grommit's request, Chalky was going to the forge where Rusty and James Sanderson served the surrounding community as smithies. Joe Grommit's message was to ask his long-time friend a favour to make a new cradle on his fire to replace the present abortive mess with a more manageable fixture. Chalky approached the forge, he was quite apprehensive about facing the Sanderson's. He had little to do with them over the years although he was one of James' peers, their friendship was cool. They had nothing in common and Chalky had an inferiority complex towards James because of his stronger position in life.

However, Joe had explained his past friendship with Rusty, and Chalky's visit to the forge on Joe Grommit's behalf gave him the comfort to deal with his request. Chalky walked towards the open doors of the Forge. Rusty and James were working a white-hot length of steel together, shaping the volume of the white-hot mass to the required shape finish. Chalky watched the dexterity of Rusty and James, his presence at the forge door was ignored as they continued with swift hammer blows beating the now red-hot work on the anvil.

The metal had lost its pliability, "Stick it back into fire, James me lad, bellow it back to its whiteness." They both looked at Chalky in the door entrance. "What's thy business, Chalky lad?" said Rusty, "James, give it some more bellow, mek it as white as thee can, another pounding should do the trick." Rusty looked at Chalky, "Thy'll have to wait till this next poundings done, lad." He looked at Chalky, "Move over there, lad, flying sparks'll not do thee any good if thee gets caught napping." Chalky stood his distance as Rusty and James finished the task to their satisfaction.

Rusty and James finished the job to their satisfaction. The beads of sweat they expelled fell from the brows of the two blacksmiths.

They were soaked up by the thick leather aprons that protected them from the flying sparks. "Tell me what's on thee mind, Chalky lad." Rusty's friendliness put him at ease, "I know its somet to do with me old mate Joe Grommit, it's known thy's been running and doing for him, that's good of thee lad. Old Joe needs propping up a bit, and it's a good thing thy's doing. I know thy's had a tricky time, its gives me a buzz of faith toward thee. I had a whiff from over't bridge that Joe wants somet fixing?"

Rusty looked at the shy faced Chalky, "Come out wi Joe's problem and the journey from the crags will be sorted." Chalky put Joe Grommit's request to Rusty. He told him his asking of his wants will be sorted. "James!" Rusty called his son. He came to Rusty and Chalky, "The things we've put by in yon corner, can't we fix Chalky here wi a few bits and pieces? How's tha doing Chalky?" said James, "Not seen thee for a fair length of time. How's your young 'en? Must be up to the shoulder by now." Chalky looked in a sheepish way at a fine-looking James. "Not been good for a long time, me ma's finding times rough." He looked at James, sadness in his eyes, "But since I've been fetching and carrying wi Joe Grommit, me feelings are good."

James indicated to Chalky, "Over ere int corner, can thee do owt wi some of this lot?" Chalky pulled amongst the offering that were in the corner of the Forge. "Tek what thee want, if there's a use for it, and for your youngen anorl." Chalky went from the forge wearing a fine hat and a good tunic which looked baggy around his slim frame. "Thanks to ya both," said Chalky, "Mr Grommit will get the message."

Chalky waved goodbye cheerfully, and went back to the village of Lime Crags swaggering in his new attire.

Chapter Five
The Market

The Acorn Inn at Ivanhoe Mill burst with life. It was market day, and the nearby village square was filled with thronging crowds and traders alike. The vast amount of wares was there to be bargained for in the happy and raucous atmosphere. James Sanderson and Katie Wainwright strolled through the market crowd; they had been walking out for some months. The limited time they had together were precious moments in time to enjoy the feeling of great pleasure they both enjoyed. They felt quite conspicuous and timid that they may be seen together.

Henry Wainwright, Katie's father the vicar of Lime Craggs, would not be amused that his daughter Katie had not sought permission to be alone without the presence of the chaperone. She was disregarding the code of her father and her strong feelings toward James was the path she had chosen. "Does tha feel easy Katie ith the way we walk out?" James looked at Katie, she gave him the answer in her shy smile, and her long blonde hair sat gently on her shoulders. The carefree look she gave James made him feel that life with Katie Wainwright was very sweet. "Would tha like one of them toffee apples?" said James, "They've got plenty of redness under't toffee."

Katie looked at the wide grin on the face of James, "It'll take a lotta licking the toffee gerrin down to the apple skin." Katie gave him a sharp nudge with her elbow, the smile and the twinkle in her eye gave him a buzz of delight. "I'll tek that red en please," said James, he handed over his penny and walked from the stall toward the Acorn Inn. James saw his father Rusty sat at the table at the outside of the Inn.

"Katie," said James, "If thy's in a mind to, I'd like you to meet father." Katie responded, "What would he think of his fine, handsome son stepping out with his lady of choice licking this?" Katie held it up to the grinning face of James, "I'm not even down to the red apple skin yet." James said, "Me father seeing a fine lass like thee wouldn't take unkindly to you eatin' that, ask him to finish it for you, he'd pleasure that." Katie gave James the dead eye, "Aw! Come on then!" she said. They went over to the table where Rusty was sitting alone. "Hi Pa," said James, "I'd like you to meet my friend Katie Wainwright." Rusty was faced with this beautiful young lady standing before him,

James and Katie sat with Rusty, Katie looked rather shy and timid in the company of father and son. "Thy's nowte to fear here, young lassie," said Rusty, "To be amongst father and son as thee is should be in comfort." Rusty's words settled her, Katie adjusted to a more comfortable position at the table. She felt rather self-conscious, still holding the toffee apple. "If holding the toffee apple is a bother to thee lassie, give it here I've a better use for it, if thy's finished."

The milling crowd outside the Acorn Inn was boisterous in their engagement of the market. The time of the day was moving on to a late period where Katie told James that they had to return to the big house. Their goodbyes were acknowledged by Rusty. James and Katie went out of the market square and made their way to Cawston Manor. They walked through a quiet wooded area on the outskirts of Ivanhoe Mill. They were more at ease away from the market square and held hands in the most comforting way as they happily made their way along the path to the big house.

Katie looked at the handsome James and felt so proud their free time in the market was the most enjoyable and a bonus for them both. James looked at his lovely prize. Katie was turning more and more into a dream of his desire and knew she was feeling the same way.

"When I leave you at the big house Katie, will thee think pleasurably of our time together?" Katie squeezed his strong, warm hand.

"If you have the same feeling as I that is my answer James." They have both expressed their pleasure of their company. They arrived at Cawston Manor and were both timid about being seen together. Careless tongues may wag and Katie's father may get an unsavoury picture of her indulgence of the blacksmith's son, James Sanderson.

James watched Katie walk quickly up the pathway to the big house between the straight parallel rows of beech trees and went out of sight. James went back to Ivanhoe mill with a gladdened heart. As James walked back to Ivanhoe Mill, the sky was darkening and the threat of a storm was in the air. James quickened his step as he headed homeward. A clap of thunder disturbed the peaceful scene. Rain was now falling heavily. James was caught in the heavy down pour but his spirit was still joyful. Katie was safely back at Cawston Manor. James was now soaking wet, but his heart was bursting with love.

Chapter Six
The Storm

Joe Grommit huddled in the corner of the shack. The ruthless strength of the wind and lashing rain rattled the rough construction of Joe's residence. The bell from the church at Lime Craggs was being tolled violently. Its amplified sound piercing through the harshness of the storm. The last time the church bell had rung in this way was during the explosion at the lime quarry, when the accident and fire decimated the area. Joe's thoughts of the experience with the death of three workmates and his own injuries were a constant reminder of that sad day.

Casper, his faithful companion was comforted by Joe. He huddled beside his master near the warmth of the fire. The strong wind and the lashing rain were constant, "Thy's nowt to be fazed about me, old beauty, things el soon be rate." Joe looked at Casper, his sad eyes gazed towards the fire as he lay curled up in comfort as the storm raged. Joe took his favourite pipe from the wrack that was fastened to the fire surround. He emptied its spent tobacco from its bowl and refilled it from his leather pouch. He lit a taper from the glowing embers of the fire. Joe's short, sharp breaths brought the pipe to life. His comfort from the storm outside seemed to be more tolerable as he watched the rising patterns of smoke slowly fill the room in the flickering candlelight.

Joe's loneliness saddened him. From time to time it put his mind to times gone by when things were more in comfort and companionship in the village. His circle of friends then kept his daily life in a pleasant routine, his brother was his only relative. They were abandoned as infants and survived by the kindness and benevolence at the time of their needs. The companionship of young Chalky Bagshaw made his daily routines more manageable. He still felt the sorrow of his bad luck, he had become a recluse and settled to his present way of life. He accepted that this was his destiny.

The storm still rattled forcefully; the fire needed feeding. Joe needed to go to the woodpile outside, he cursed the fierce storm. He opened the shack door and shuffled the Woodstock filling his container. The strong wind made his task awkward; he entered the safety of his shack and breathlessly closed the door behind him.

Joe fed the dying fire with his fresh fuel and did his routine of domestic chores. His thoughts were returning for the night. He thought maybe he could sleep the night away; the storm may subside later.

He settled into his bunk; Casper lay at his feet on the coverings of Joe's cosy nest. The candles now extinguished, the wind still howling and the fire losing its comforting glow. Joe Grommit tried to settle for the night. The church bell still echoed through the harsh surroundings of the storm. Casper sat at Joe's feet, and the fire embers lit up the small areas around the room. Joe moved restlessly under the coverings of his bunk. The bell, why the bell, a storm wasn't any reason to ring the church bell. Joe's thoughts were puzzled. Why is the bell tolling? As Joe lay with more comfort now in his bunk, faint sounds of barking dogs were heard.

"Something was wrong down at Lime Craggs, the morning will give me the answer," thought Joe. The sound of barking dogs was constant as their presence broke through the sounds of the storm. Joe lay with the thoughts of the commotions that had been ongoing for a long time into the night. "There's nowte to be done till things have settled," Joe said in the comfort of his little nest. "We'll stick wi where we

are till morning, old lad," he laid his hand on Casper and tried to settle.

Casper was alert, his low growl constant, his head raised and looking toward the shack door. Joe sat up on his bunk, "Thy's heard somet, lad," Joe felt uneasy as Casper still growled in his long drawn out message to his master. Joe put his hand on Casper's head. "Steady old lad, has the wind spooked thee?" Joe cocked his head listening for any sound that had troubled Casper. Just the stormy confusion disturbed the night, maybe that had sparked Casper into the alert of the goings on outside.

"Settle now lad, tha's note to fear, nowte at all whilst tha's wi me." Joe lay down in his bunk leaving Casper still attentive at the door to do his own thing. Joe tried to settle into comfort, he felt that the storm was relenting a little. Casper lay quiet on the floor next to the door expelling small growls that seemed to trouble him outside.

The persistence of the stormy night went on and on. Joe left his bunk, went over to the near dead fire and fed it with a few fresh sticks and brought it back to life. He filled his water vessel, "Tea is calling Casper lad, here, get thee teeth into this," he threw Casper a well chewed bone he kept out of his reach and treated him with its comfort. "The night is moving slowly, Casper," Joe looked at his beloved companion who now wrestled with his second hand bone.

Joe sat at his table; the room now warmed up a little as the fresh fire flames did their comforting job. Joe's next comfort was his pipe, its faithfulness in times of want was always there… Tea and pipes were good tools to use when the chips were down. He and Casper shared the troubled night together with the hope of a better day. The flickering candle light adding to their feeling of loneliness and the puzzled thoughts that troubled him of the happenings in the stormy night.

Barking dogs and voices outside, Joe's shack alerted Casper to respond with his natural reaction that he heard beyond the door. "Joe Grommit," the voice outside the shack was answered by Joe who was trying to settle Casper, "What's the bother at this hour?"

"There's things I need to ask thee, open up Joe," said the voice outside. "Just a few words of asking," Joe lifted the wedge from the door and faced the constable and dog handlers that had aroused him. "The bother we've brought to you Joe is that we've had a raid on the docks at Lime Craggs, we are looking for some culprits that have escaped our detection." Joe replied, "Nowts been seen by me constable," Joe held the door part open, looked at the scene outside, the rain still lashing down and the rough wind contributing in its own unpleasant way.

"Thy's a bad job to sort out lads," said Joe, "There's nowt I can tell thee, all I heard was the Lime Craggs bell tolling, wind and lashing rain, upsetting the peace of night!" Joe faced the drenched pursuers of the criminal gang, if thy's a mind now to constable I'm shutting up, good luck in the quest to find what thy's looking for." The constable thanked Joe for his indulgence and signalled his departure. Joe secured the door, the problem at Lime Craggs had now been explained. He sat at his table by the dying fire. "We'll try and get to morning, Casper. The best way we can." Joe finished smoking the last of the live backy in his pipe and went to settle in the corner of the shack.

Joe settled in the coverings of his bunk. Casper lay his heaviness on the legs of his master. The storm still prevailed as the night moved slowly to a new dawn.

Suddenly, Casper went to the door, barking furiously, "What's the bother now, lad? Thy's so het up tonight, settle thee sen!" Joe looked towards the shack door, only darkness was in the room, "Come here, lad, thy's heckling me now wi all the fussing about." Casper was still active at the door.

"Joe, Joe Grommit," a voice on the outside unsettled him. His senses were dulled with the tiredness upon him. The voice outside the door called Joe's name again.

"Open up Joe, its Josh Tetley, thy'll not be fazed by me calling in on thee," Casper continued his aggression at the door. "What's the reason for callin' Josh?" Joe waited for his reply. "Let me in tha's nowt that'll harm thee," Joe opened the door holding his dog back with his foot. Josh Tetley stood before him; his rain saturated state was diminished to a state of desperation. Joe was an old friend of Josh, there was no fear in him. He could handle the man before him on his own terms. "Come in, lad. Thee looks in a right state," said Joe as he looked at the soaked figure of Josh Tetley. "Calm down, Casper old lad, I've got the job sorted." Joe lit a candle its flickering flame chasing away the darkness, "Seeing as thy's soaked to the skin Josh, thy had better fill the wood bucket." Joe held the empty vassal to Josh, "Fill her up, life in the fire will soon be rate again, then we'll sort thee saturated self out." Josh went to the log pile at Joe's request, the fire soon got to its warmth. "Don't tell me why tha's here till we've sorted thee out, things have been uppity all night, your visit at this hour don't matter now, get thee togs off, thy must be raw to the bone!"

Josh did his musts and got into a more comfortable state, his teeth chattering visibly, the new blazing fire did its job, "A drop of tea is not to be sniffed at Josh," he looked at his now more settled visitor, "Good man, Joe, thy's still the steady kid from the past, what I've got to tell thee won't be as sinful as thee might have in mind."

Joe looked at Josh, his tough appearance and commanding personality was now diminished. He now looked comical in the dry garments that Joe gave him. Joe was fully alert now, this moment in time was just another part of his long night of happenings. The dawn will soon be here, Josh shivered close to the now blazing fire. The welcome comfort of the heat subsided in the shivering Josh, "Thy's a good en Joe," said Josh, "Thy's been in my corner a few times when things have got sticky for me in the past." Joe looked at the now downtrodden figure of Josh Tetley. "I've watched you rise and fall over the years lad," said Joe, "Thee keeps mixing with bad lots, thy's not smart enough to tek hold of thee senses at times." Josh looked glum as he listened to Joe Grommit. He knew his words were right, the truth of this wild night was brought home to him.

Joe Grommit, his long term pal spoke the words that was Josh Tetley, "Get this down thee lad," said Joe passing a can of hot steaming tea to Josh, " I'll be straight with thee about the happenings of tonight Joe, but I want it kept here in the shack."

"Whatever tha speaks about," said Joe, "Stays here. I don't want me sen mixing with any bother that goes on at Lime Craggs. I rough it out with the state I'm in now, but if they leave me as things are, I'm settled in my mind."

Josh told Joe of the cause of the raid that took place at Lime Craggs. Loaded boats that were to be shipped to their destinations with cargoes of valuable goods. A raid had been arranged and I had been drawn in with the promised rewards. I know that things for me have gone uppity at times. I was sucked into the web again, that is why I'm here with you tonight, Joe."

"I know there's treachery," said Joe, "Thy's got to cover thee back lad, or thy'll finish up being locked up for good."

"When things are sorted tonight, Josh, thy stopping here must be kept wi us alone lad." Joe looked at Josh Tetley huddled round the glow of the fire. "If it gets out that tha's been covered by me, I'm in bother."

"There's note that'll do thee harm Joe," said Josh, "Thy's done fine for me tonight lad, they'll be made up with goodness for the way thy's looked after me." Josh looked into the fire; the steaming wet garments were straddled around the confines of the room by the coming of morning.

"Another can of tea," Joe filled Josh's empty vessel, "it's still howling out there, lad," said Joe as he looked at the forlorn figure of Josh Tetley. His strutting and confident personality now looked in a state of dishevelment. "No chance of any kip tonight lad," said Joe, "Does tha still have the likes of young Rosie on thee mind Josh?" Josh looked at Joe, a wry smile on his stubbled face. "A warm lay beside Rosie would be a fair swap for the likes of tonight," said Josh, "She's a good en, that lass." Joe looked at Josh as he stared into the fire, his big hands clasping his tea. "There's note wrong wi Rosie, nowt at all." Joe looked at the now settled Casper, "I've got my cuddles here." Joe scuffled the head of his canine friend, the contentment enjoyed by the warmth of the fire.

"What's the plan as come morning, lad?" said Joe, "I hope thy is covered thee sen as to what thy was up to when things kicked off last night." Josh faced Joe, "I've a mind to do a runner for a while," said Josh, "There's no trust around that lot that's done tonight's Job." Josh had a scared look on his face, "Thy'll be snitching and squealing all around. I'll get me sen parted from here, I've a place to go Joe lad." Joe felt Josh's plight was a sorry state to be in, "When it comes for you to go lad, do as thee has to." Joe looked at the anxious face of Josh Tetley, "When it's time for thee to go, do as thee mind teks thee and keep thee gob buttoned of ya visit to me." Josh gave Joe his assurance that his visit will never be revealed.

Chapter Seven
The Boat Trip

A bright sunny day was a pleasure to be enjoyed, it was midsummer. Life in Ivanhoe Mill had a joyous feeling, the village residents looked in a contented mood. Rusty Sanderson sat outside the forge at Ivanhoe Mill, he was having a friendly banter with two of his neighbours. "Work is slack and hard to come by," Rusty chatted in his pleasant, friendly manner. "I've told my lad James to scoot for the day, get his sen off we his lassie, there's not much brass coming our way." Rusty finished his banter with his friends, and went into the Forge.

James had planned his day with his lassie Katie, they had planned the hiring of a boat, today was for him and Katie alone, the pride of his life gave him a buzz of excitement. His thoughts of anticipated pleasure that the day might bring gave him such a good feeling.

At Cawston Manor, Katie had made arrangements to have the day in company of James, she had saved up the time owed to her and was given the time to suit her request. Emily, Cawston Manor's housekeeper, over time, had a caring attitude for Katie. She spoke kindly of her and her father Henry Wainwright, the vicar of Lime Craggs. This is where she attended the church services. Emily had seen the romance of James and Katie blossom since she had been employed at the big house. Katie had confessed to Emily that her father had a strict code of ethics that his she had to obey. Emily condoned the courtship of James and Katie, it gave her a feeling of motherly connection she enjoyed, the role she played, it gave her pleasure. James made his way to Cawston Manor, a spring in his step and a good feeling in his heart are what he carried with him to meet the most precious person that had come in to his life.

James arrived at Cawston Manor, and waited at the entrance. Katie soon appeared walking down the road that lay parallel to the two rows of Beech trees. She was holding a basket which swung gently to the rhythm of her steps. "Thy's a sight to set me heart pumping lass," said James. Katie handed James the basket, "Emily sends her wishes for a pleasant day," she said, "All the goodies are there, let's be off, this day is for us alone."

They walked toward the river that was situated by the Acorn Inn. They would take the hired boat to use at their leisure on this most beautiful day that had been bestowed onto them.

They were now walking along the tow path; the river was busy with various craftha. A heron on the river bank tussled with a fish he had caught and was manipulating it to a comfortable position to swallow its prize. James held Katie to a stop, "That's a fine sight my sweet lady," said James.

He pointed to the heron on the bank of the river. "Everything has its own method of eating," said Katie as she held James to the closeness of her, he squeezed her warm and tender hand with pride. "Thy has caused a good feeling in me, Katie lass." They watched the heron devour its prey and continued along the towpath to the boatyard. The sweet flowers in the hedgerows and the scents they gave were abundant. Nature was so giving, and a cherished delight.

"How does thy feel, my sweet lady?" said James, a call from a passing boat prompted a friendly wave from Katie, "A good feeling is upon me this day," said Katie. "The likes of today have touched me in such a fine way," said James. She held him to a closeness that warmed him to such an awareness, they stood in the seclusion of the tow path, their guard was down and their natural feelings could not be held back. Their eyes spoke together, their lips touched in the tenderest way. This was their first kiss. They both stood back from each other, hands were clasped, their smile acknowledged the beauty of their experience. With a deep sigh of satisfaction, Katie looked longingly at James that faced her, her cheeks flushed with a deep pink glow that added to her natural beauty. "Hold the basket, James," said Katie, "This fine walk needs us to share the weight of the picnic." James with an affectionate squeeze of Katie's waist, picked up the basket of goodies. A fallen willow tree across the towpath had to be manoeuvred. The tangle of branches restricted their path, they passed the fallen tree and were soon in front of the boatyard where they would pick up their hired craft. They passed tethered boats and crafts that sailed the river.

They acknowledged the good mornings with busy crews exchanging happy banter. This was a welcome reward that brightened the day. "Good morning to you, Freddie," James and Katie were in the hired boat moorings to pick up their craft. "Good day to you, young James," said the boat attendant, "How's that fine blacksmith father of yours?" James answered Freddie, "I just left him in good spirit," said James, "And who is this maiden of desire that accompanies thee on this fine day?"

"This is my friend, Katie Wainwright, the daughter of Henry Wainwright, the vicar of Lime Craggs." Freddie looked wistfully at the handsome couple standing before him. "Happy day you must have with the company of one of my trusted boats, just take great care, be shy of the other river crafts and thy safety will be in tact when you return at the days end."

"Thank you, kindly Freddie, I'll tell father of your kindness, and if thee wants any favours with the boats you know where we are at."

James and Katie waved goodbye to Freddie, the small rowing boat packed and ready for the expectant day ahead. James had used the hired boats on numerous occasions. He had assured Katie that she was in good hands, James looked with pride at Katie's as he pulled strongly on the oars. "Thy looks in fine fettle, my sweet lassie, keep the eyes ahead and keep the rudder in your control." Katie looked admiringly at James, "Yes captain!" she chuckled with pleasure as she maneuvered the boat down the river. This was a new experience for Katie with her control of the craft. Katie giggled with delight at the praise of James. "You could give me a promotion my darling, what task would I have to perform to make me more confident?"

James looked at Katie with a glad heart as they glided swiftly down the smooth waterway, they had travelled away from the moored craft that busied the village of Lime Craggs. The quiet beauty of the surrounding countryside stood in all its glory. "Emily has treated us with some special goodies," said Katie. "If they are to the sweetness of my lady," said James, "They'll give my palate a treat."

"Your palate was treated on the tow path when you stole the kiss." James stopped rowing letting the craft drift slowly down the river. "They cheek of you!" said the grinning James. The thoughts of his first kiss was such a tender experience. He looked at the beautiful young Katie with a glad heart as they drifted peacefully down the river.

"The sweet talk is a torment Katie thy'll finish up in clasped irons with thee mutiny." James looked at Katie in a serious manner, "Tek hold of thee sen lass, thy's near the bank you'll have us in the water." James pushed on the craft with his oar taking the craft into deeper water, "I'll have to put thee on a charge of negligence." James put on a serious face but Katie dismissed his comments and pulled a face at the now grinning James. "The lock will soon be in sight," said James. "We'll have a break from the water and skag around the woods for a bit," Katie nodded with delight. "We can sample the treats from Emily," said Katie, "The taste buds may have more delight than the kiss," tormented Katie with a look of mischief on her bonny face.

They steered the boat to the mooring before they reached the lock which was a short distance ahead. "A fair spot is this, my little Katie, thy work on the boat is deserving of Emily's treat," James tethered the craft, and helped Katie and the basket of goodies onto the river bank. The boat was safely tethered on its mooring, James and Katie sat on the grassy, sloping bank facing the calmness of the river. Katie looked at James. "The basket," she said, "it's between us." The mischief in her was aimed at James and the basket. Katie moved the picnic basket from between them, James took his liberty and moved close to his smiling lady.

"James," Katie looked at her young companion, "If thy'd like to warm thee lips on mine, it's what I'd like thee to do." James clasped her hand gently, leaned over to his beautiful lady and kissed her tenderly. "Shall we try some of Emily's basket now?" said James, "There's a hunger in me, I hope you feel the same."

"The hunger is with me, also," said Katie. "Does food and kissing go together James?"

"I can't think of anything to match it!" replied James.

The contents of the picnic basket were enjoyed by James and Katie. Even the wildlife on the river was treated to a portion of their goodies. They splashed and fought for every crumb; Katie squealed with delight at the frenzied sight before her. "Oh James," said Katie, "This day will go into my memory as one of the treasures of this wonderful day..."

"To me, my sweet Katie, every day spent with thee lass is time that'll be there forever." They both looked at each other and both knew it was a moment to finish their picnic in the tenderness of embrace. "Enough of this pleasure," said James, "We could scout about in the woods, does thy fancy that pleasure Katie?" said James, "If I am with you my darling, there's note that I feel could be better." They cleared the picnic area and took a short walk into the wooded area that was set back from the river.

The sweet-smelling scent of flowers was a bonus that added to their day, bird song was all around and the chorus of different species echoed their sounds intermittently and was another pleasure. "James look," said Katie, "That's a kingfisher."

"We are looking at a creature that matches thy beauty my sweet lassie, has thy a notion where we are Katie?"

"I'm not to know as where we are," she replied. "This is part of Cawston Estate." They were suddenly confronted by a bearded thick set man, "What might thee be doing on this land?" The threat in the man's voice dulled the pleasure they were having. "Begging your pardon sir, my friend and I were only strolling in the pleasantry of the wood."

"Thy's on private land, me lad. I'm the game warden to Cawston Manor, I can, if I've a mind to get you in bother. His lordship is troubled with poaching." James looked at the game warden, "Begging your pardon," said James, "We are not here to trouble thee at all, I am the son of Rusty Sanderson, the black smith at Ivanhoe Mill, and Katie my lassie works at the manor." The game warden looked in a fairer way at the young couple. "I'll not put thee in bother this time, you know now where thys at when thee comes in here, you best be on thee way, keep your side of the boundary, and keep thee sen rate."

The sun warmed the pleasure of the day as James and Katie sailed down the river towards the lock. They wanted to finish the last part of their boating experience to keep as a special memory.

The lock appeared in the distance, barges and river crafts moved in both directions as they passed James and Katie. Friendly banter and waves of acknowledgment, as they passed, were signalled to them, their small rowing boat rocked from side to side. The ripples of the passing craft, giving a more robust feeling in comparison to the smoothness they enjoyed.

Katie dragged her hand through the water as James pulled gently on the oars. "Thy's day dreaming lass," said James. "To be stranded would be a misfortune for us way out here!" Katie looked at James, "Are you chastising me captain?" she looked at James. "Stop whittling I'm in full control at this end," she threw a splashing of water scooped from the river at him. "You have just been awarded a penalty of 50 lashes for your cheek," James said to Katie, "So is that why I'm to be punished?"

"Thy'll get your sentence when you pull in," Katie steered the boat towards the mooring. "Katie, Katie," shouted James, "Thy's lost it again." Katie had steered into a tangle of overhanding branches and debris at the edge of the river.

"Thy's beached us good and proper." James was tangled in the web of growth; Katie shouted her apologies as James tried to escape from his plight. Katie was panicked, the boat rocked dangerously as James struggled, James passed an oar to Katie. "Try and push it at the bank as I am." Katie did as James said, "Push, push, that's it lass, keep doing as you are." The boat was slowly moving out from the bank, they moved from the branches that held them in its web. "Hold thee sen steady, Katie," said James, "I'm sad for thee that what's happening spooked thee lass." James was now comforting his shaking little lady.

"The blame is on me, Katie." They both sat in a quite dishevelled way looking perplexed at each other. James held Katie gently, she needed his gentleness. Things were now calm. Suddenly from the tangle on the river bank, a bulbous shape rose from under the branches. A vile aroma was coming from the object. Katie screamed in horror. James held the terrified Katie to him. They both knew it was a body.

The boat drifted slowly away from the submerged body into the centre of the river. James still held Katie in the comfort of his arms. Her distressed state concerned James as he tried to settle her. "We must go to the lock," said James, "Can you handle your rudder?" Katie nodded; James carefully guided her to a position where she could steer. "We go to the lock," said James. They were soon composed and set off toward the lock in the distance, they tied the boat to a mooring on the river bank. James assisted Katie from the boat, "Lock keeper," shouted James, "Show the sen if thee's in."

James looked for a sign of the keeper, "Wait here Katie," said James, he went up the steps of the lock house and opened the door. "What's all the shouting about? Tha's upsetting me kip young 'en, what bothers thee?" James told the keeper of their tragic find down the river. "There's a craft on its way thy'll have to wait while I send him through the lock and sort it art wi him. That best I can do, lad." James thanked the keeper, and went to Katie telling her the situation. "Don't whittle about our plight, we can make good of our day together," said James. "There's bother for me," said Katie, "Me father will not tek kindly to the happenings of the day James." Katie looked at James looking for some supportive comfort, "Thy's gonna be rate lass, thy can't be hung for enjoying yoursen, it'll all blow over, things el soon be as sweet as a nut!"

James held his sweet lassie in the comfort of his arms, the barge was entering the lock, and the lock keeper had words with the barge master, pointing to James and Katie. He came to them on the lock side. "Tha's had a shock as thee," said the barge master. "Down yon," pointed James, "Tha can ride wi me to yon spot, we'll do what has to be done."

"I'll come wi thee," said James, "My lassie will stay here."

"That's no bother wi me laddie." James told Katie that he was to go with the barge master. He would be back when they had sorted the sad event they had witnessed in the river.

James left Katie with the lock keeper and sailed to the spot of their discovery. As they neared the location of the body, James had a thought in his mind that it could be Sam Lister who went missing in the harsh hours of the past winter. "Slow now," said James, "Over yon, amid the overhanging branches."

"I see, I see." The barge master pulled to a stop beside the submerged body. "Pass me the pole," said the barge master to James, pointing at the long pole on the top of the barge. James watched as the body was hooked by the pole. "We must reverse the craft back to a safe stop." James held the hooked body secure as the barge reversed to a more secure part of the river. "There's note more we can do now. We'll make him safe.

James looked distressed at the bloated body. Even though he couldn't identify the corpse he was quite sure it was the missing Sam Lister.

They secured the body, the barge master thanked James and sailed on his journey to Lime Craggs. James went back to the lock, to the waiting Katie. She found comfort in his return. James explained what he and the barge master had done with the corpse. It was now time for them to sail back to the boat yard at Lime Craggs.

They passed the location of the body, where it had been secured on the banks' side. A group of people were minding the scene waiting for the constables to organise the removal of the body. James and Katie passed the scene of their discovery and sailed back to the boat yard. Word of their discovery had got back to Lime Craggs, the barge master had given details of his actions to the appropriate authority. James and Katie arrived back at the boat compound; Freddie was waiting. Their craft was the last hire boat to be returned to the security of Freddie's care. "Thy's had bother down at the lock lad," said Freddie as he guided James and Katie to the safety of their mooring. "Finished our day in a bad way!" said James.

James looked at the distressed Katie, "We'll have to face the music with Henry Wainwright! His lassie being on the river with me will be a problem for poor Katie."

"What's done is done laddie," said Freddie, "As long as thy's finished the day sound, nowte can harm thee now."

James and Katie acknowledged Freddie's good luck, and made their way back to Cawston Manor.

James left the anxious Katie at the entrance of Cawston Manor. He watched her walk slowly towards the big house. The picnic basket she carried didn't have the carefree swing as when she met James at the start of their day. Katie waved to the waiting James as she walked up to the big house to vanish out of sight at the end of the parallel twin row of Beech trees. The following morning arrived; Katie faced Emily. Her enquiry had to be explained. She knew that Katie and James had planned the picnic, but the trip on the river was not in their mention of the day. "Now then, Katie," Emily looked at Katie's nervousness, "There is much to be explained of the day you and James spent together, the master has heard of some misgivings that have displeased him." A tearful Katie was at Emily's disposal to take the wrath of her tongue. Her silence at Emily's aggression had stunned her to silence.

"Mr Cawston is displeased with the events of yesterday, some answers have to be explained. The trip on the river was unacceptable and has to be explained to your father, the fact that you cannot swim had put you in the possible danger of problems that may occur. You are in care of Cawston Manor, and we have a responsibility to keep you safe! However, your picnic has had unsavoury misgivings, you and the irresponsible James must give satisfactory answers to your father and Mr Cawston. I will leave you with your thoughts and explanations."

Katie was in a tearful state, "Wipe the tears now, Katie, you will be seen at Mr Cawston's convenience to explain your actions of yesterday." Katie with her head bowed in silence, nodded to Emily in her sorrowful state. "Off to work now young lady! Mr Cawston will send for you at some point in the day, come along now, and pull yourself together." Katie turned away from the chastising Emily and walked out of sight to do her chores in the manor. Katie's expectancy of being called to confront Gunston Cawston had not arrived. A few anxious days had passed, but no word of her recent picnic was mentioned. Emily's mood as she went about her duties, keeping the house running in her own bullish way, was quite normal.

Katie was still troubled in her mind waiting for her call to face the music. James had been, without the knowledge of Emily, in contact with Katie. She had briefed him with the news that she was to face the master and explain their picnic adventure. "There's nowte that can't be handled wi out gerrin het up about it lass." James held Katie gently in his arms. "Just pass things off wi out gerrin thee sen in a state." James reassured Katie, she seemed more at ease. His comforting had made her more settled. "Thanks, my precious darling," said Katie. She looked admiringly at her beloved James. "Go now, gerund wi things as they come." James left the embrace of his beautiful friend. Katie went back to the big house with the comfort of seeing him making her day more tolerable.

As the days passed without any incidents of confrontation that Katie had expected, she felt that her past worries had been forgotten. Emily was more approachable, and treated Katie in a fair and pleasant manner. Katie had spoken to James, and he thought that things had been cast aside to be nothing but a past memory. Unbeknown to James and Katie, Henry Wainwright, the reverent father of Katie had been visiting Cawston Manor for the last few days. Katie had not seen or had any notion of her father's visits. Emily was sworn to secrecy about the visits of Henry Wainwright. She escorted Katie's father to the confines of Gunston Cawston's quarters and briefed about the calling of Henry's visits, and was instructed to make sure Katie was not around when her father visited the manor.

Emily viewed the visits as very mysterious. She put her eavesdropping techniques discreetly to work. What she was hearing from small snippets of conversation between Gunston and Henry was so puzzling. The conversation from what she picked up named James and Katie at various times. Emily was trying to piece things together but she could only assume parts of their meetings. She knew the visits of Henry Wainwright would eventually bear fruit. When it was time for Katie's father to leave the manor after the meetings with Gunston, Emily was called to the library and instructed to divert Katie away from any part of the manor where she might see her father leaving.

Only slight contact was made by Henry Wainwright towards Emily on these occasions. Even though she worshipped at Lime Craggs in his constituency, he was tight lipped in the manor. Emily had a friendly rapport when she attended his services. She thought it safer to maintain her friendship with the Vicar and leave any meddling at the Manor alone.

James was feeling puzzled that no contact had come from Katie at the manor. He had tried to contact her in several ways, but to no avail. If he could find Joseph, who assisted James when he did work at the manor, he would ask him if there was a problem. James still had the same feelings of desire and happiness towards his beautiful Katie. He felt sure that she also felt the same way.

He must find Joseph, who worked at the manor, to find the reason for the absence in what was happening to their beloved relationship.

Rusty and James were hard at work in the forge at Ivanhoe mill. James pumped the bellows that fetched the iron work in the white-hot fire to its consistency of redness. Rusty was aware that James was not handling things in his usual way. He seemed to be otherwise engaged. His mind was elsewhere. "Has thee got a problem that bothers thee lad? Thy's not been thee sen lately. Spit it out if thy has. Tha's lost thee concentration. What's up wi thee?" James looked at Rusty, his silence prevailed. He was looking for a way to explain his anxieties. He didn't want for his troubled mind to look that he couldn't handle his affairs. "Let's knock this lump of iron into shape now lad, its good and hot to be worked." Rusty indicated for James to put the white-hot iron work on the anvil. "A wet of tea open thee up to get out what's on thee mind, I can't have thee moping abart like a sick dog. Come on, finish off this iron work, then we'll have a man to man enquiry as to what's bothering thee."

Still in silence, James finished the job with Rusty. He filled the billy can with water. "*Maybe the break will open me up,*" thought James as he made the hot brew. *"Being unsettled like this wants to be sorted."* James was still tight lipped as he handed Rusty his tea. After their break, which was taken in silence, Rusty and James looked at each other in anticipation that James with his sullen mood could be analysed and talked to Rusty of what bothered him.

"Nah then, lad, if thy's a mind to, lets know thee bother in that head o' yours, thee can't be moping like thee is, thy's gone all to pot overt last day or two." James looked at Rusty, looking for a way to reply to him. "I have had bother in me mind father, for a few days." James looked at Rusty in a sad way, Rusty knew that his son had a mood that he didn't recognise. "Spit thee bother out lad," said Rusty, "You're doing me head in with all this stuff thy's showing me, if thee minds messed up, get it off thee chest." Rusty put his hands on the shoulders of James with a gentle assurance, he looked him in the eye waiting for a response from James. "Come on lad, fire will be dead before thy opens the gob as to what's wrong wi thee, gerrit out you're doing me ed in." "There's bother in the big house," said James, "Since our trip on the river, and finding the corpse of Sam Lister, there's been bits of chat that's bothered me." James looked at Rusty, he had opened up now. Rusty was anxious to conclude what bothered James who now felt more at ease.

"Say it as it is, lad," said Rusty, "That's how to sort the job out." Looking Rusty in the eye, James started to say his piece. "Since our trip on the river, there's been things that's not making true as to what happened on that day, apart from bits and pieces that me and me lass Katie did. Why has things gone sour on us? The big house is quiet of my wanting to see my lassie. No wrong was done by us and no word from the big house about Katie." Rusty took in the words of James and calmly sucked at his freshly filled pipe of backy. "If thy's done nowte to unsettle folk, me lad, thy's no fear to worry. If thy wants to bottom the bother, that's mekin a stress wi thee, go straight to the bother that's niggling thee and take it from there."

James looked despairingly at Rusty, "It's like hide and seek, Dad," said James, "All this messing about and not knowing things that's under wraps needs sorting." Rusty tapped the spent backy from his pipe, "Now thy's opened up lad, all I can say to thee is this, find out the happenings with the absent words, and ask Katie straight out, 'What's happening at the Manor?' Tek it from there, that's all thee has to do at this time, if thee gets no joy, get to yon big house and say tha piece." James pondered on the words of Rusty, "I'm trying a way first of me own," said James. "Young Joseph who works at the manor, the lad who Mr Cawston sends to me when I work at the big house, I'm hoping to get a word to him, and find out from Katie about the silence that I'm bothered with"

Rusty looked at James, "If thee wants to leave it at that lad, so be it, tek things as they come, it'll all come out. Mark me words, lad. There's always a solution that'll always come out into wash." The following afternoon, James had time off from the forge. He was intent on pursuing the reason of the silence that had been troubling him.

He knew that Joseph, who worked at the Manor, had free time from his employment. He hoped to confront him and glean some information as to why Katie had forsaken James with this upsetting silence. He knew in his heart it was not her intention not to see James. What had turned the tide of this mysterious silence was out of character as to the piddling day out which to James and Katie's mind was quite normal.

James set off for Lime Craggs which was over the river from Ivanhoe Mill. As he walked along the lane to the Craggs, he saw Chalky Bagshaw walking towards him. "Good day to thee, Chalky. Good day to thee," he nodded to James, "Where's thee off to? I see thy still dons the tunic I gave thee a while back." Chalky grinned with a cheeky smirk, "A bit of alreet this, James. It's a rate gift thy's given me."

"Suits thee Chalky, how's thy youngen?" said James. "Me ma's troubled by him, can't do owt wi him, always in bother. "Chalky," said James, "I am going to Lime Craggs to find Joseph White. Have thee seen owt of him around the craggs?"

"Not seen him these last few days," said Chalky, "As around thy'll flush him out." James acknowledged Chalky, and continued his journey to Lime Craggs.

A fair bit of action was happening over the bridge, horse and traps taking up the narrow lane, going back and forth to Ivanhoe Mill and Lime Craggs. Plenty of pedestrians and activity going about their business. James acknowledged a few friends and acquaintances on his way to the Craggs to seek out Joseph. The main street in Lime Craggs was still in a state of disrepair near to the site opposite the end of the village, where the disastrous explosion and fire had devastated a large part of Lime Craggs. He knew Joseph lived on the edge of the ruined part, it was a short distance from the church and rectory, where Katie's father lived.

James walked quickly past the church and rectory, a few of the villagers were going about their daily tasks. No sight of Katie's father was in his sight. He reached the end of the village where the damaged buildings, which were still in a state of disrepair, stood. Joseph lived on the edge of the ruins. His father was badly injured in the explosion at the time of the disaster. He died a few months later, his mother and her children lived and struggled in a fair amount of poverty.

Joseph was the eldest child, and Reverend Wainwright looked after the family in his benevolent role. He was responsible for finding employment at Cawston Manor for Joseph.

James came to Joseph's cottage, which was at the side of the ruins that was destroyed by the disaster. It looked in a state of poverty, James felt a sadness that the White family had fallen onto hard times. It made James feel rather content that he was in a more settled state. As he walked to the door of the cottage, a dishevelled young boy faced James. "Now then youngen," said James, "I'm after a word wi your Joseph, is he knocking abart?"

"Who's calling Arthur?" the lad looked at James, "A big kid is wanting Joseph, Ma." Mrs White came to the door and faced James. "What's the business wi me lad?" She looked at the handsome James who stood facing the sad looking Mrs White. It made James feel uncomfortable at the poverty he was seeing before him.

"He's gone to yon Craggs, look for him ya sen, I'm mixed up here wi me own carry on, ask around a bit, thy'll find him hangin' about."

"Thanks," said James as he walked from the White's cottage.

Young Arthur ran after him, "Mr," James looked down at the young lad, "I think our Joseph's gone to the Craggs He helps Chalky Bagshaw. They get eggs and things." James looked at the young lad, "Can thee tek me to find him?" asked James, "I'll gi thee some pennies." The beaming little face of Arthur shone with delight. "Al go get me boots," he ran indoors to get his feet coverings. "I've told me ma," said Arthur, "I've to watch me sen and do as thee tells me." He took the hand of James, "Come wi me, I know a short cut to the Craggs."

James was being tugged by little Arthur, "Steady on youngen, thy's no need for thee pulling at me, tek thee time." Young Arthur relaxed his grip on the big strong arm of James. They made their way along a narrow path toward the wood in the distance away from Lime Craggs Quarry. James and young Arthur reached the end of the narrow path which took them to the outer perimeter of Lime Craggs. They were now on the edge of the wood, in a quiet end of the Craggs.

"This way Mr," said Arthur as he tugged at the hand of James.

"OK," said James, "Thy's no need to pull me along." James looked around the thick wooded area. "Is that Joe Grommit's place?" said James nodding toward a shack on the edge of the woodland.

"Ve that's Grommy's place," he looked up at James, "I'm not scared of Grammy, I've been with our Joseph a few times, he's not scary to me now, he likes me, I run abart for him, he giz me things and knows me mam. He worked wi me dad before he was tecked from us after what happened to him." James held the hand of young Arthur, "Come on, lad," said James, "Tek me to Mr Grommit's place."

"Can I have some pennies Mr, after we have done?" said Arthur as they walked towards Joe Grommits place. "'Course you can lad, let's find your kid, I'll gi thee some pennies, before thee goes home to thee ma."

They reached the shack where Joe Grommit lived. Casper, his dog came toward them, barking with aggression at the two figures. They stopped at the entrance of the shack; the dog still barked. Joe Grommit came from within, he shouted to Casper, "Curb thee row, lad." Joe settled his dog and looked at James and Arthur. "You must be looking for somet round ere, me lads." Joe Grommit scowled at James and young Arthur, "Thy's Rusty Sanderson's lad, ain't thee?" Joe looked down at young Arthur, "What's tha doing wit youngen?" James looked at the disfigurement on the face of Joe, "Looking for Joseph White, his nipper youngen thinks he knocks about wi Chalky."

Joe leaned on his wood chopping bench beside his open shack door. "They be back soon I hope, what's in thee mind as wanting to see him?" said Joe. "Just a bita bantering I want to sort out," said James. "While thy's ere lad, tek a look at the cradle on me fire you fixed me a while back." Joe went inside the shack, young Arthur fussed about with Casper, tormenting him with a stick. James looked around the primitive furnishings inside the shadowy interior. The flames from the fire cast intermittent shadows around the dull room. Joe pointed to the fire cradle that James and Rusty made a time back.

"Thee and Rusty did a fine job for me, youngen, but can tha see that back end?" Joe pointed at the fire cradle, "It keeps leaning over when I put any weight on it." James nodded at Joe as he pointed at the cradle. The weight ont front end is unsteady, can thee see me meaning? It wants sorting at the back end," said James. "I can see what thee means Joe." He looked at the young blacksmith, "Can thee do owt we it?" said Joe. "Send Chalky to the forge, I'll mek it safe for thee," replied James. Casper, who was playing with Arthur outside the shack, started barking.

Chalky and Joseph had returned from the wood. James greeted them, "What's thee doing here wi our youngen?" said Joseph, "Just had a walk ova from the forge, I've a bit o' time to spare, young Arthur fetched me over to see thee, Joe's found somet on his fire cradle, he wants a bit more fixing to it to mek it safe. Chalky can fetch it over to the forge when he can." Joseph looked at James, "Has thee been to my place?" asked Joseph, he looked at young Arthur who was still tormenting Casper with a stick. "I went over to see thee about somet that bothers me at Cawston Manor, young Arthur brought me here, he said you'd be here wi Chalky, if thy's a mind too, I'd like to ask thee as to what's bothering me." Joseph looked with interest at the sadness on the face of James.

"There's note wrong wi a chat if there's owt I can help thee sort out, I'll be glad on it, said Joseph. "If thy's things to do here at Joe's we can chat when thy's done here." Chalky opened the bag he brought back from the woods with Joseph. "Brace a nice jack rabbits today, Joe." Joe had a satisfied look on his scarred face. "Thee can gut 'em and stretch the skins,"

Joe looked at young Arthur, "Maybe mek a hat for the youngen." They all had a bit of friendly banter, the rabbits were gutted and skinned ready for the pot. Joe looked at Joseph, "Thee tek one for thee ma, lad. Thy's done well for me." Joseph showed his pleasure, "Thy's doing me a good service you youngens, we have Mr Sanderson with us today, he's to fix me cradle."

Joe looked at his young company, he had satisfaction on his face. James, Joseph and young Arthur went from Joe Grommit's shack. They walked the narrow path through the crags toward the home of Joseph and Arthur. James had given Arthur his promised pennies, he ran ahead of his brother and James, delighted with his prize of pennies. As they walked together, James talked to Joseph about the silence from Katie at the big house. He wanted information and if he had the opportunity, could he speak discreetly to her. James was so worried about her silence, "I know that Henry Wainwright has been visiting quite often," said Joseph, "No word has been spoken about any problem at the manor regarding Katie and her father, no contact has been seen with Katie and reverent Wainwright. Emily seems to keep Katie busy when his father comes to visit Mr Cawston."

"Joseph," said James, "You must help to put my mind at rest."

He looked appealingly at Joseph, "As a friend, please talk to Katie, try and arrange a secret meeting at the stables beside the manor. We have met there many times before. I am sure she would agree to my request, I know she would." James held Joseph's arm, "Do this for me Joseph."

"I will, I will do as thee wants me to," said Joseph. "Thy has to keep things quiet as to me being part of you asking to help thee." James assured Joseph no word would be spoken about the request. They came from the crags to the cottage where Joseph lived. "I'll leave thee now," said James, "Do as thee can for me, they'll get thee reward my friend." James walked back toward Ivanhoe Mill with hopes that he could find a solution to his problem.

James arrived back at the forge. Rusty, hard at work, was sweating profusely as he hammered a white-hot block of steel into shape. He glanced at James, "Thy's a mind to show the face has thee," shouted Rusty. "Thy's just in time to gimme some of the labour if thy can spare it," said Rusty sarcastically. In silence, James donned his apron, Rusty indicated for his son to put the now cooled work back into the fire. He started pumping the bellows vigorously as Rusty waited for the return of the iron that James was bellowing to its workable temperature.

Still in silence, James passed the white-hot iron to his father who looked displeased that he had to struggle without the assistance of his son. Father and son completed the work together, and stood silently with their backs to the now simmering fire. "A brew is what tha needs father," said James, "It'll bring tha simmering temperature down." Rusty looked at his lad in a more calmed manner, "OK, son. I've struggled a bit wi thy absence, working the bellows and doing t'angle work together put me in a bothered state." He looked at James with a more apologetic face, "We'll have that brew lad." James was more settled at Rusty's calmer state.

The forge was now in a better atmosphere, the work in the forge was finished for the day. The fire embers were glowing gently, the end of the day activity was done, and peace was now prominent. "Did thee sort the problem out lad that thy's been wittering about?" said Rusty. James looked at his father, wondering if he should share his problem that bothered him. "I sort of fixed a few worries," said James, "It'll be alreet if I can get sorted to me liking, if thy wants to know the bother that's had me rattled, I'll tell thee, if thy's a mind to listen."

Rusty looked sympathetically at James, "Come on then, lad. Thee can't go on performing like thy is. Spit thee bother out, I'm here for the lad." James nodded, "Gimme a few days,

I'll know then if somet comes of me trying to get an answer to the silence at the big house.

Rusty hung his leather apron at the side of the dying fire, "Thy get home, lad. I got business to sort out at the Acorn Inn." James nodded at Rusty's words, "Fix thee sen somet to keep thy belly full." Rusty locked up the forge. Work ended for the day.

Chapter Eight
Discussions at Cawston Manor

Rain had been falling steadily through the night. The morning sky was dark and threatening. A strong wind added to the unpleasantness. Henry Wainwright drove his horse and trap toward Cawston Manor. His frequent journeys were becoming a tiresome nuisance to his routine. His meetings with Gunston Cawston needed to come to a conclusion. He was anxious to get the problems of their discussions finalised. He snapped the reins on the rain soaked back of his struggling horse as he steered his trap through the entrance to the big house.

He reached the top of the long gradient and pulled his horse to a stop next to the stables. The groom had been waiting for Henry. He helped him from his trap. Henry acknowledged him gruffly. His mood was rather sharp. "Sorry for my sharpness," said Henry to the groom, "This terrible morning has quenched my mood." The groom took charge of the horse and trap. Henry went to the side door of the Manor, where he was received by Emily. "Good morning, Vicar," said Emily, sarcastically. Henry stepped inside the dullness of the interior. He took off his soaked cape and hat, handing them to Emily. "Thank you, my dear," Henry grimaced, his discomfort showing on his face as he handed his dripping garments to Emily. "They will be in a more comforting state when you leave, Vicar," she said. Henry acknowledged with a grunt of approval.

"I would like a short while to settle," said the Vicar, "Before I see Mr Cawston."

"Then I will serve you with a warm drink," Emily indicated for the dishevelled Vicar to follow her to a quiet guest room, she passed the wet garments to one of the house maids, "Do what is necessary my dear," said Emily to the maid. "Have them warm and dry when Mr Wainwright leaves later in the morning," the maid departed to attend the order from Emily.

Another day of seclusion in the quarters of Gunston Cawston was to be enacted. Emily's ears, she hoped, would be tested to glean any information from the closed doors in the confines of the meeting place with the vicar and Gunston Cawston. She had eavesdropped whenever she could about the contents of their meetings and had formulated a picture regarding their confrontations.

Emily was very intrigued with the snippets of planned negotiation that had come her way. She was aware that her eavesdropping was unethical. But her quest to satisfy her nosiness was her prime aim.

After a few days of James meeting up at Lime Craggs with Joseph, there was still a silence from the big house. James had begged Joseph to make contact with Katie. He felt a rejection that was now causing anger. His feelings and thoughts gave him a kick to his pride. James thought, *"Katie can't be interested in my attention. The time lapse is getting longer. I am of no interest now. Even if Joseph made any arrangement for us to meet, I feel we have lost each other. Its maybe best to move on."*

James had left the forge telling Rusty that he had arranged to see Joseph. He was to meet him as he made his way to his employment at Cawston Manor. James saw Joseph coming toward him on the narrow lane from Lime Craggs. "I've waited in hope, Joseph, to see if thy's fixed what I asked thee," said James. "I've seen the lass," said Joseph, "There's no talk as to any word about thee and Katie."

"Look Joseph, my anger has built up to a state that's rattled me into not caring one way or other." Joseph looked agitated at the rising aggression of James.

"I saw Katie when I left the manor last night." James asked, "About what?"

"Asking that I have a message from you, and Katie looked taken aback from what I asked her. I told her you want to meet her at the stables, and she said she would let me know. Katie was nervous, and asked that I didn't speak of you, and made me promise as she didn't want to be found out. She looked wet eyed and anxious," said Joseph. "Do as thy has to with your meeting, if she can't do as I ask then forget the meeting I asked for."

"I will, I will James," said Joseph, leaving James, and making his way to Cawston Manor.

At Henry Wainwright and Gunston Cawston's last meeting, Emily heard a slanging argument from the two men and the discussion was Katie. Emily had been stunned to silence at the content of parts of the conversation.

She was now beginning to understand why Henry Wainwright had been coming from Lime Craggs to collude with Gunston Cawston. She had done the receiving and departure of the reverend as instructed, and, of course, Katie had always been absent from the sight of her father when he attended the meetings.

Emily had picked up part of an aggressive argument about the birth of a child that had been born at Lime Craggs many years ago. The continuation of this argument was suggested by Henry that the child had been conceived at the manor when the mother had been employed there. Gunston Cawston and Henry were expressing their points of view as to the fathering of the child. Rumours that had been hidden for so many years were discussed. The child's mother had been sent to an alternate employment at the estate of Gunston Cawston's uncle many miles from Lime Craggs.

The child had been reared by the benevolent charity of Henry Wainwright. As the child grew up, Henry Wainwright assumed a fatherly instinct to the girl, Katie was the name that was mentioned in the discussions. Emily now had an interesting piece of the picture she could put together. That explained the arrangements of Katie being kept secluded with the visits of Henry Wainwright. Another exciting fact that the discussions had uncovered is that the mother of the child had a very close relationship with the Vicar.

"This is our final meeting Henry; Katie has accepted her move to my uncle's estate. Let's close the matter and move on, we both know it's for the best and Katie will, I am sure, be the true beneficiary. You know and I know, Gunston, what had happened when Katie's mother became pregnant, and even though you have denied it for so many years, your conscience has opened a little door in your mind that tells you what I have known over the years. There is a likeness that is undisputable, and is plain to see and also the way you have warmed to her during her employment at the manor. It is such an indication of you knowing the true circumstances of Katie's birth. The fact that you made such speedy arrangements for the child to be looked after by my benevolence proved to me that you were in denial. That the fathering of Katie was down to you! As much as I accept your argument Henry, it's only your unproven thoughts that have brought you to the idea that I am the father of Katie."

Henry spluttered angrily at Gunston's fervent reply, "For goodness' sake, enough is enough!" Henry looked exasperated, "You have won the favour of your plan to do what you selfishly have planned." Henry looked defeated as he stared at the smugness on Gunston's face. "It is the most agreeable solution," said Gunston. "If you can finally agree, I will contact my uncle Sebastian Dangerfield to come to the manor and take Katie to work in his employ." Gunston looked at the defeated Vicar, he nodded solemnly in silence, "You have been difficult to deal with Gunston, let it be on your head if this taking away of Katie from my care takes on a sour outcome!"

"Have hope, Henry," said Gunston, "We shall overcome any unsavoury aspects that may lie ahead." Gunston rang the bell for service. Emily appeared. Gunston requested refreshments. Emily took the request gracefully, Gunston Cawston breathed a sigh of relief.

James waited at the end of the lane that lead to Cawston Manor. Joseph sauntered casually from Lime Craggs to his employment at the big house. "Has thee got what I asked thee?" said James as he confronted Joseph, "All I can tell thee is this, there's as few rumours about Katie. I know the vicar has been coming to the manor."

"Then tell me what thy's picked up," said James, "Did the see Katie? Did thee mek a plan to meet at the stables? James looked at Joseph's disinterested attitude. "I did ask, and told her of you wanting to meet at the stables, I'll let thee know later. I'll see you at your place tonight, I should have somet for thee then." Joseph left James; his attitude had turned into couldn't care less. He walked back to the forge to do his daily routine; his interest was diminishing. He could feel that he was being separated by the happenings at Cawston Manor.

Gunston Cawston had settled his plan with Henry Wainwright as to the immediate future of Katie. He had to get word to his uncle Sebastian Dangerfield, and ask for his cooperation to take Katie into his care. Sebastian was aware of the facts regarding the birth of Katie at the time of her birth. They had both colluded in the sending away of her mother. She had been in Sebastian's employ ever since the birth to avert any scandal that was aimed at Gunston Cawston. Henry Wainwright was also implicated at the time of Katie's birth; he had a strong relationship with Katie's mother.

He was intimidated at the time by Gunston and Sebastian to send the mother back to the estate of Gunston's uncle. They had both put extreme pressure on Henry so that he would escape any scandal that may harm his position as the vicar of

Lime Craggs. To avert any fuel being cast on the present arrangements to have Katie installed into the care of Sebastian Dangerfield, Gunston Cawston had decided to act swiftly. He will request his uncle Sebastian to sow the seeds for the transfer of Katie to be placed in his care. Gunston's intention was to interview Katie to tell her that in the best interests for her future, her father and himself have decided to send her to the state of Sebastian Dangerfield, and that it would benefit her in many ways and put her in a most generous and compatible environment.

It would suit her outgoing personality. She would get a generous amount of valuable education that is surely a suitable prize that will sort her transfer to the Dangerfield estate. These events that Gunston had formulised, must be activated on immediately. He has sown the seeds; motion is now the prime action. No, faltering is not the way forward. The transfer of Katie into the care of Sebastian Dangerfield is now settled in Gunston's mind. He felt proud of his manipulation of Henry Wainwright as he sat smugly in a relaxed mood drinking a toast to himself.

The arrangements that now had prominence in Gunston Cawston's mind were to take affect by Katie being interviewed in the quarters of her master. He had made his decision to explain his intentions to go ahead with his plan to transfer to Sebastian's estate. Paramount in his mind, was to exercise care to Katie that the benefits that were on offer would sway her to favour Gunston's proposal. His uncle Sebastian had been sent a request by Gunston for him to pick up Katie at his earliest convenience. A discretional silence was arranged, he informed Emily that he would need her cooperation with Emily to keep her under strict management when he had explained to her about her impending change of employment. Gunston gave Emily the diluted facts of Katie's transfer to the Dangerfield estate, and that he needed her duty of silence.

Katie nervously stood before her master as she entered his study. He sat relaxed in his favourite chair; his hands were clasped in a comforting pose resting on his stomach. He looked at the beautiful Katie and with an assuring smile, told her to be seated. "You must not feel nervous or in fear of this meeting Katie," his smile gave a more relaxed assurance. He maintained his smile, and the calmness of his soft voice made her feel in quite a friendly atmosphere. "Are you feeling at ease, my dear?" said Gunston, he needed her to feel completely in tune as to the offer he was to propose to the young lady who sat before him.

"I have a proposition my dear Katie that I have in mind, that I know will change your life in such a magical way that I feel you will accept my generous offer to you." Katie listened in silence, "What may you be asking of me, your Lordship?" Katie looked at Gunston Cawston who was now in a more serious attitude. He still showed the same comforting assurance, she waited for his next words, "How would you like to live on a fine estate, where you would have the facilities of education and recreation of a lady?"

Katie took in the words that were said by Gunston Cawston. "How can you offer me such luxury? I am only a simple house maid in your employ," said Katie. "I and your father have been in consultation for the last few weeks, and we have both been in the same order of mind that if you were to accept our proposal, it would give you excitement and a purpose in life that must be an offer you could not refuse to accept." Katie was bewildered, she looked at Gunston's assuring look, "You must consider the proposal I have explained. Think on my words Katie. This is a life changing offer, let me know tomorrow of your decision."

Katie arose from her chair, "I am rather taken aback by your words, my lord. Will my father be present if I take the decision of your offer?" Gunston looked at Katie, she was looking for some sort of support.

"Trust my faith in you, Katie. I will make an arrangement to satisfy you as to what is the best thing to do in your own interest." Katie backed slowly away toward the study door, "Your request will be granted, my dear." Gunston watched her departure, his thoughts had a pleasantness of pride. He rang for refreshments and prepared to write to Henry Wainwright.

Even though Gunston had success from their meetings, he just needed clarification in the eyes of Katie of her father's approval.

Over the last few weeks, the discussions between Gunston Cawston and Henry Wainwright which had taken place, Katie had not been home to stay with her father. She had stayed at the manor as a maid at her father's request. In that way, it was kept from her as to the plan of her move to live at the Dangerfield Estate. James had been strong in her thoughts, she felt that the absence of not seeing him was her father's doing.

Joseph is the only connection with James that had reached her. A chance to meet him at the stables would prove difficult. She had told Joseph that if there was any chance that she could meet and see him, she would let him know as soon as possible. If they were to meet, what would be the reaction of James if she told him of her master's offer of moving away to the Dangerfield estate many miles away?

Katie had given great thought of the fact that the absence between them had been done in a deliberate way, she was sure her father and her master Gunston Cawston were responsible. Emily had been lacking of her usual friendliness, she suspected the change in her attitude had been influenced by the master with his plan to have her moved away from Cawston Manor. She had to explain what was happening at the house.

Katie's confusion and conflicts in her mind troubled her. The offer of a new exciting life at Sebastian Dangerfield's estate was certainly a strong magnet of opportunity to accept.

Telling James of her departure would be such a painful way of telling him that her choice had been made by the collusion of Gunston and her father. It was going to be inevitable, the pressure on her was the road she would have to take. The hurt that they would both experience, she knew, would be distressing in the most painful way. Katie would contact Joseph to arrange a meeting at the stables at the first opportunity so that she could clear her mind that had mixed up her emotions so dramatically.

Gunston Cawston received confirmation from his Uncle Sebastian that he would arrive at Cawston Manor in the next few days.

Katie was to have her belongings and her domestic attire from her home at Lime Craggs and the Manor ready for transportation to her new home. No secret meeting between Katie and James had transpired. She had no opportunity to make that happen. Her master had further talked with Katie in the most pleasant way. He went into details as to what duties and additional things that she was offered. The educational and social life at the Dangerfield Estate was a puzzling aspect of why a mere maid, such as she, was to take part in what was a clear indication of her role in her new life.

Gunston Cawston assured Katie that she had performed her duties so well in his employ that he felt sure she was worthy of a much greater scope with her natural abilities and personality. Her master's ideas were cast in her mind, which made her suspicious of a possible motive for all this interest of planning what had happened. Katie had challenged the additional things that she was offered, but she was assured there was a genuine reason for the role she was to play at the Dangerfield Estate.

"I want you to be settled in your mind, Katie. In the next few days, your life will take on a new meaning for the better," Cawston's words were listened to with anxiety by Katie. His explained vision to her was out of her scope of the expectancy that she would be capable of in her new role of life at the

Dangerfield estate. "I hope not to let you down," Katie looked for assurance as Gunston nodded with a reassuring smile. "Go about your duties my dear, be strictly silent to the household about our discussion." Gunston Cawston watched Katie depart from his study. His satisfaction was in place, he rang the bell for service.

Joseph stood outside the forge door waiting for Rusty and James to start their daily work. He had arrived at their workshop on his way to Cawston Manor, before the two blacksmiths arrival. Rusty and James looked at Joseph who walked toward them. "What's thee ere for at this time of day Joseph?" said James, "Is thee after tekin on some graft?" Joseph looked sheepish as he pulled James to one side and Rusty unlocked the forge door. "I have a tale to tell thee, James, that thy'll bei 'n ager about." Joseph looked at James standing a few steps away anxiously, "Come on then, spit thee words out. By the looks thy's showing a load of rubbish is what thy's gonna spout at me."

James looked at the pathetic expression on Joseph's face, waiting for his furlong excuse that had been ongoing for so long now.

There were no positive results coming his way, "Say what thy's got tucked in thy head, then on thee way. I have some graft to ger on wi." James waited for the words Joseph had come to tell him. "She's gone. Katie's gone!" he said. "Gone where?" asked James, "Thy'll be gone if thy don't come out wi some sense." James looked at the stuttering Joseph, "The uncle of Gunston Cawston has been at the manor, name of Sebastian Dangerfield. It's all happened in a sudden way." James grabbed at Joseph's tunic, "Now thy's saying she gone?" Joseph pulled away from the grip of James. "Took by thee uncle of Gunston Cawston last night. Katie's gone to his place, miles away. It's all been hushed up."

James looked at Joseph with a look of anger, "Thy's done nowt for me. All thy's done has faffed abart. Nowts come my way from thee." James pushed at Joseph who slowly backed away from him. "On thee way to thee work. I'll find out what's to know in me own way." Joseph walked quickly away from the forge. James answered the call of Rusty, a bad start of the day has just been given to the now angry James.

A spell of silence from James continued. Rusty looked at his son, "Come on, lad, spit thee bother out. I know thy's bin bantering wi thee mate from the big house. What's spooked thee anger?" James found no words to answer James question, "When thy's ready, come clean wi me, there's note that can't be settled." Rusty accepted the silence, he knew the problem of James would come. They both went through their daily chores in silence.

"I'm putting me problems to rest for now, Dad. When I've sorted me sen out, I'll get on wi telling thee what's messed me about, o'ert last week or two." Rusty nodded, "Let things be put by for now. When thy's got rid of thy anger, you can spout out the problem." Rusty scruggled the hat on the head of James, "I'm having a swig or two at the Acorn tonight. Thy come wi me, tek thee mind from the hurt thy's showing." James agreed to Rusty's words.

Chapter Nine
The Boisterous Acorn Inn

Activity and boisterous pleasure filled the Acorn Inn. It seemed that the whole village was taking up with the enjoyment all around the smoke-filled room. The residents of Ivanhoe Mill were certainly filling their boots with the pleasures that were all around them. Charlie Horner, the landlord, was in constant demand. The clambering for his services was constant. The music from. Pepe the entertainer and his magic fiddle penetrated its dulcet tones through the noise of the boisterous crowd.

Rusty, James and his friends had acquired a prime spot around the comforting fire. Their tankers were filled with requests from Rusty's table as their bantering through the noisy room was difficult to decipher. Rosie served around the room, she squeezed and manipulated her way through the crowd as their demand was satisfied. In the company of Rusty and James, was the dog belonging to Josh Tetley. Rosie had looked after him since he disappeared after the robbery at Lime Craggs. Arrests happened after the crime; the Acorn Inn had been a crime scene that was used as a front to plan the robbery. Charlie Horner, the landlord had been exonerated from any suspicion.

Rosie, although she was an intimate friend of Josh Tetley, escaped any involvement of the crime. Charlie Horner had cleaned up the Acorn, any suspicions of unfair dealings were dealt by him and his selected friends with very deft philosophy. Rosie, had a yen for Rusty, and since the absence of Josh Tetley, James had an instinct that her friendliness had been happening between them. He hadn't mentioned to James of any involvement. Rosie had also taken on the looking after of Tilly Blagdon, since the tragedy of losing her family in the terrible winter of the past.

If Rusty wanted James to know of any spark between them, he had the respect that he would be told by Rusty. At this moment in time, he would leave it dormant. Rusty also had an interest in the welfare of Tilly Blagdon. He had supported Rusty since the tragedy, between them, they had been her benefactors. James thought that maybe the reason for their friendliness was looking after the welfare of young Tilly. James and Rusty were making a move to retire from the company of their friends. James fussed the dog of Josh Tetley that had been in a placid contented state. He soaked up the gentle attention and savoured the titbits of snacks that came his way. Rosie was in a more relaxed mood. Her task of keeping the customers happy had now slowed to a minimum. The now sparsely populated room was coming to the end of its merrymaking. The ale had done its job of creating a mixed night of social integration.

Pepie sat quietly in a corner of the room playing his violin in a gentle way to a small group of friends who were enjoying the pleasant end of the night, listening to his popular melodies.

James and Rusty were stood with their backs to the dying embers of the fire. Rusty was offering a light to his freshly filled pipe. Rosie came over to James and Rusty. A much-used cloth laid over her shoulder. She looked at Rusty and nodded her head at James who was giving his last cuddles to Josh Tetley's dog before they went home. "Has the had the spunk to spit things art to him Rusty?" James was still fussing with the dog. Rusty pulled Rosie a few feet away from James. "It's telling him at the rate time Rosie," said Rusty. "Is thee sure that thy's in thee state thy is?"

Rosie with a sharp repressed grimace answered Rusty's doubt to her problem. "Thy'll see the sureness in a shorter time than thee thinks." Rusty looked at James who stood near the dying fire talking with a friend. "Is tha ready to be off, Dad?"

James had his fill of ale and was feeling mellow. His night at the Acorn Inn had settled his sadness of the news that Katie had gone from his life. Rusty took a sharp pull on the stem of his pipe, expelling the smoke slowly. He looked at Rosie, then at James. "Be with thee in a sec, lad," said Rusty. He gave an assuring look at Rosie, "It'll 'appen, Rosie, gi me a bit longer, it'll all be done and dusted."

Rusty turned to James, "Let's get home to a bit of snap, lad. There's brass to earn fo't pot tomorrow." He looked at Rosie, "Things will soon be rate, lass." He touched her cheek gently. Rosie recoiled from his touch, "Show us thy's no coward, and I'll give thee some credit." She watched Rusty and James depart from the premises. Her feelings about the future scared her. Her intent was the making of the commitment from Rusty to happen, and hope it would put her in a more secure state. The thought that gave her the most fear is what Josh Tetley would say about her infidelity.

Joe Gromitt tendered to his domestic routine in his shack. He was sparking new life into his fire. Casper was chewing a well-bitten bone. The noise outside disturbed Joe and his dog. Casper barked at the voice beyond the door, "Is tha at home Joe? Open up thy's nowt to fear. It's the constables."

"What's thee wanting of me?" said Joe. "A few words about the robbery a while back." Joe opened his door slowly holding on to Casper's collar. "There's nowt I can help thee wi, lad. They called on the night as was the crime. Shook me up thee did." Casper still growled at the constables through the partly open door. "There's been a few things turned up that you might have a knowing of."

"There's nowt I can tell thee one-way ort' other," Joe still held the door partly ajar. "If thy's in the clear Joe, open up. Then thee can get on with what thee need to."

Joe opened his door. "You best come in. I'll settle thee queries best I can," said Joe. "We'll come straight as to what's on our mind." The two constables looked at the nervous Joe Gromitt. "Some articles of interest were found in the wood a short way from here." Joe snapped angrily, "What might these things be as thee's asking of me? Say thee peace, man and leave me to get on with me daily doings!"

The constables looked with interest around Joe's shack, "Thee knows of Josh Tetley. Don't thee?" Joe faced the two constables. "Known him since he was a young sprog," said Joe. "What's he to do with me? Not seen him since me accident. I'm hold up here. Don't see many folk round abart."

The constable stared at Joe looking for a flicker of guilt. Joe evaded the penetrated stairs from his visitors. "No showing here of Josh you say or since the crime you're saying you haven't seen him."

"I've said me peace," said Joe. "That's all I can tell thee." The constable looked at his partner, "Okay, Joe. If we need to see thee again, we might give thee a call." Joe nodded as they closed his door.

Joe was troubled in his mind. Could it be that word had reached the constables of Joe harbouring Josh Tetley? If they had him in their grasp, would he squeal on Joe? He gave his word that his lips would be sealed on what had happened on that stormy night.

The forge had been busy since early morning. Rusty was nursing a kick from a horse they had been shoeing. James finished the task for Rusty, and the horse's groom gave his assistance to James. "Somet spooked him Dad," said James. "I'm losing me touch lad," said Rusty. James and the groom finished the shoeing of the horse and coupled him to his cart seeing him on his way from the forge. James tendered the injury to Rusty who gave him some comfort with a covering on his injured leg. "Put things on hold for now, lad," said Rusty, "Boil some water—a brew is what's needed." Rusty's grumpiness with his son looked prevailed as James prepared the brew.

Tea and a thick cheese sandwich were a welcome break they had earned as their morning had come to a halt. James had a mind to mention to Rusty about their suspended talk from a while back that Rusty had promised to discuss. The injured Rusty may not be ready to be the advisor to James at this moment in time. He decided to let his past problems slip by for now. James was enjoying his regular visits to the Acorn Inn with friends from the village and Lime Craggs that satisfied his social life. Katie's memory was fading into the distance. Maybe, he wouldn't need to bother Rusty with the past. He would sort his own feelings out in his own way.

Rumour and speculation were a common discussion at the Acorn Inn. There had been arrests and dangerous talk of the robbery at Lime Craggs that had put a number of suspects in fear of accusation. Josh Tetley was sought after as a serious ring leader.

If he was in the clutches of the constables, there would be fear in the village of repercussions that would terrify anyone with something to hide. Rosie was in the frame. It was common knowledge that Josh Tetley was her woman. The rumours about him disturbed Rosie. Her present problem that she had to endure was that Rusty Sanderson was now connected to her. Rusty was having to shield himself from the small talk that was aimed at Rosie. His friendship with her would cause many snippets of gossip when the true facts came out of their relationship.

Rusty was spending more and more of his free time at the Acorn Inn. He was spending it with Rosie. Tilly Lister, who lived with Rosie at the inn, was kept busy helping Rosie with her domestic work. Tilly was maturing into a fine-looking young lady under Rosie's protective custody. Rusty had kept up to date with Tilly's welfare at the inn. He had an empathy with the young lady since he rescued her from the terrible snows of the past winter. James had suppressed any comments of Rusty's continued social time that he spent at the Acorn. He was becoming involved in a way that was causing gossip, and which was to James an embarrassment. He felt he could hold his tongue no longer. It was strong in his mind to tackle his thoughts and find out the true value of their relationship.

Rusty felt in a more settled mood. James was in the picture with his relationship to Rosie. They had settled in to a routine which suited them both. A message came from the big house, "James," said Rusty. "Cawston has a few bits and pieces for us to fettle." James listened with a nonchalant attitude. He was still wounded with contempt for the big house, and its shoddy doings of what had happened to Katie, "I've lost the yen to think about the manor," said James. "We still have to banter with their wanting of us to do what's needed lad," said Rusty. "The big house keeps us fed and watered. Thy'll have to grin and bear thee hurting of what's been and passed. I'll go and see Cawston in a day or two. We need all that's needed to keep the brass coming in." James replied in a cool manner, "Do as thee must. I know thee has to cow tale to Cawston." James pumped the bellows bringing a fierceness to the bright roaring fire.

Things were quiet in the forge. Rusty had made arrangements with Gunston Cawston to offer his services at the manner. He felt uneasy about confronting Cawston. They had many skeletons in the cupboard, which went back years. He knew that one day the outcome of the past would have to come out into the open. It would surely put his life and that of James in controversial turmoil. Rusty wasn't ready for the eventual outcome of the past. When the confrontation with Cawston takes place, he has to be clear in his mind that he can handle the past.

Rusty knocked on the partly opened door. Emily had seen him walk up the drive. She waited to greet the fine looking

Rusty. She had always had a respect for his honest way of life since Katie and James had developed a friendship. She had encouraged what has grown between them but since the past weeks with the transfer of Katie to the Dangerfield Estate, Emily had to change past feelings for the couple to suit her position in the manor.

"Good day to you, Mr Sanderson," Emily greeted him with an awkward smile. They shook hands respectfully. "Good day, Emily. It seems such a long time of seeing you!"

"Come inside, Rusty." He entered the hallway, "Let me refresh you with a beverage before you meet Mr Cawston. He's not available at the moment." Rusty followed Emily to the kitchen.

Chapter Ten
Friends on the River

Rusty Sanderson had spent a number of days at Cawston Manor making arrangements to complete outstanding work that was ongoing by the Sanderson's. Rusty was tight lipped about his visits and evaded the questions of James on his return from the big house. He pacified him nonchalantly. James tried to read between the lines of Rusty's replies but let things lie after getting no joy from his father. "Thy's done some good graft, lad," said Rusty as he proudly looked at his son. "Thy can tek some free time and do thee own thing for a couple a days." Rusty looked at James waiting for his reply. "Thy's a rate sweat on today, lad." James stopped the pumping of the bellows, looked at Rusty and nodded breathlessly as he took the white-hot metal from the forge, handing it to Rusty.

"I'll tek thee up on that!" said James, "A fine thing thy's said father. A thing I've not told thee abart is offered by Freddie. We do bits and pieces on his boats down the river moorings. He's offered me any social doings for me pleasure on his moored boat as a payment for looking after his wants." Rusty was pleased for his son. His words satisfied him. It would give him the break he needed to put his disrupted domestic life in order. There was too much haggling and complications that were finding their way into Rusty and Rosie's relationship. Things had to be simplified, too many sharp tongues were bandied about and giving cheap pleasure to any listeners of gossip that was aimed at Rusty and Rosie.

He wanted a settled mind so that his plans for the future with Rosie and young Tilly Blagden could be settled. He had offered Rosie his commitment of a safe and protected relationship. Rusty had planned in his mind that it would seal his thoughts and benefit the outcome to his satisfaction.

James and friends were socialising in a mixed group. The lads and lasses banded and prattled happily. James was jovial about the leisure they were looking forward to on Freddie's boat.

James had been in the company of a lassie who had taken his fancy. She had accepted his offer and James thanked her for his request. She lived at Lime Craggs, and was a friend of Katie. He suspected that she knew of his relationship with her. No word had been mentioned since she had been in the company. Rusty entered the room, he walked towards his friends who offered him a seat at their table. He acknowledged them with a friendly smile. Rusty settled with his friends, his fresh filled tankard of ale was swilled down with relish. "That's a fine start to the night," said Rusty, licking his frothy lips. "What's the crack toneet, lads? What's thee got in thee heads that's wanting to be sorted, there's a few in here toneet that wants a sorting out, Rusty lad." Rusty looked about the crowded room, "I can see the local Scragg has a nest of listeners, it's like a group of earwigs waiting for the local scragg to fill their lug holes wi a load of rubbish. She spits out of that venomous spout that never stops working."

Rusty's table of mixed smiles acknowledged Rusty's remark. "She eye-balled me as one of her preys when I put me foot into the door," said Rusty, "Felt her fangs click straight at me throo'et." Rusty bared his neck, "See thee here. Thy can see she's into me." They looked at the table of Bessie Hardy. She had felt the vibes from Rusty's table but her poisonous spouting was already at work. Her listeners were gleaning the gossip that Bessy was feeding them with relish.

Rosie was at work among the customers. She looked tired and forlorn as she struggled with her work load. Her pregnancy was now prominent. Charlie Horner had given her added assistance. Rusty discreetly eyed Rosie's presence as she worked amongst the customers. She assured him from time to time that things were okay. The night carried on to its conclusion and started to thin out. James and his friends had settled their plans for the boat venue. Pepie as usual, played the evening to its close with his beloved instrument. James went over to Rusty, telling him he was to see his young lassie friend home to Lime Craggs.

Rusty went over to Rosie. He reassured her that he had made some constructive arrangements for the future.

She was more settled in her mind that Rusty had made a firm promise to look after her and the child in an honest way. The night concluded. Charlie Horner did his ushering out of the pub, thanking his friends and customers with his usual pleasant wishes. He thankfully closed the door with a sigh of relief.

"Take care of the boat that's in thee care," said Rusty, "Gimme wishes to Freddie, tell him we've time for his business anytime." James waved to his father. It was good to have freedom. James had thoughts of anticipated pleasure in his mind as he made his way to Lime Craggs. He was to meet his new lassie, Hilda. She had accepted the proposal of James to be his partner on Freddie's boat. James and Hilda were to be joined by two other friends from the Craggs. They were to meet at the tow path that led to Freddie's boat. James had planned to stay on the boat overnight. He was looking forward to fishing and maybe a swim.

James reached the tow path. Two of his friends were waiting. Hilda was missing, and James was disappointed, "Hilda is to come at a later time. She says sorry," said Tommy. They looked at the disappointment on the face of James, "We'll get on without her then, as thee got the snap for the stay?"

"Ay, lad," said Tommy, "I've got somet you will like to share later," said Poppy. A cheeky smile lit up her bonny face. "We look forward to your surprise then," said James.

"Let's gerron to't boat, it's no good hanging abart waiting for Hilda." James looked so disappointed, "She might show up later, it's up to her." They walked along the tow path toward the boat to meet Freddie. Friendly horse play by the three friends set a happy atmosphere as their casual walk took them to their destination where Freddie's boat was moored. The day was warm and full of summer beauty. A rich array of wildlife was a pleasure to behold. Tommy and Poppy walked ahead of James, thoughts stirred in his mind, when he took this same walk to the boat compound when he and Katie were to spend the day on their beautiful picnic. The drama and the outcome of finding the body of Sam Lister had turned joy into a sadness.

James thought that he had put an end to his relationship with Katie. He felt an annoyance as he started to think about his relationship with Katie. He vowed to clear his mind and forget about the time he had spent with the wonderful love of his life. He had vivid aspirations of the past, but as her absence over the months had passed, he had mellowed with the thoughts of Katie. This walk along the tow path made him sad. His memories of the past were hurting him. He had started the day with hope of pleasure. The absence of Hilda as his chosen companion had hurt his confidence. James was now of the opinion that Katie did not have the same amount of feeling for him as he had for her. He knew he had to settle for the present, and his self-annoyance must be swept away.

They arrived at the boat yard, where Freddie was organising his hire boats for the day's business. He greeted the friends with jubilant enthusiasm. "Good day, me hearty's," shouted Freddie as the three youngsters stood at the mooring, "Now then, Freddie." James hailed his friend who was balancing around on his rowing boat and pulled them in order ready for hiring. "Has thee fettled thy boat thee promised us?" Freddie pointed to a mooring down the river. "It's down yon, in a fine quiet spot, thee can mess abart in comfort, do thee picnicking and such, it's at the disposal. Thee can sleep there toneet, the boats thy'ne. It's to be looked after with respect." James assured and replied, "Thy'll have no bother we'll be dead rate wi thee Freddie lad."

"Be with thee in a sec, old darlings," Freddie gingerly stepped from his rowing boats that were now safely secured and ready for the daily hire. "The keys to me boat," said Freddie, handing them to James, "Have a fine day on the boat. If thy hits any bother, get thee sen out of it." Freddie smiled with mischief. He looked at the three friends, "Vote the sen a captain and play by't rules. If thee gets any insubordination, there's a plank on't top of the boat. Use it to walk the victim into't water." Smiles came from the three friends, "Thee can come over for victuals if thy's time, Freddie," said Tommy, "It'll be our pleasure to treat thee."

Poppy's contribution to Freddie was a hug and an infectious smile. "Off now wi thee then, if thy's in any bother, thy's only to come over and thy'll be sorted out." Freddie saw them off towards his boat then tendered his doing of the day ahead.

Later in the afternoon, Hilda appeared. Freddie brought her over to the boat. James was fishing. Tommy and Poppy were exploring in the nearby woodland. James was surprised to see Hilda. There was no enthusiasm from James of her coming at this late hour. "Is thee offering the company to us?" said James with sarcasm. Hilda looked hurt, "It's not my fault I am late, James," Hilda was tearful with her explanation. "To stay the night on the boat, I had to manipulate my absence from home that's if you really want me to do as thee wanted."

James wanted his day to be pleasant. He looked at the tearful Hilda and mellowed to her distress. "If thy's fixed thee being here tonight lass, thy's welcome by me! Does thee want some goodies from the picnic?" Tommy and Poppy had a snack a while back. James was in a more refreshed mood.

Hilda's appearance has lifted the mood of James. They sat on the riverbank together, and tucked into the remains of the picnic.

Tommy and Poppy came back to the boat. They acknowledged Hilda's presence, making pleasant banter between them. They told James they had decided not to stop the night on the boat. Poppy didn't feel comforted being untruthful to her kin folk. James and Hilda decided to stay alone. James made his mind up from the start of the day that he would stay on the boat. Tommy and Poppy left their friends alone and went back to Lime Craggs.

James and Hilda enjoyed their seclusion on the boat. The idle chatter was very stimulating. James found many interests in Hilda's vocabulary which suited his lively mind. Hilda had lived in Lime Craggs all her life. She was the only child of her widowed mother. She had been nurtured and well looked after; she was outgoing and had an ability of discussion that James found down to earth and easy to mix with his own outlook on life. "Thy's a cool lassie, Hilda. I hope thy's no regret sharing thee time wi me. If thy's a feared of us being together as we are, I can tek thee back to the Craggs." Hilda looked with a smile on her bonny face at James. "Nothing would have stopped my wanting of this time together James." She held his warm hand gently. "This is a dream to me, ever since we met at the Acorn Inn." James squeezed her hand he held in her lap. "I felt a stirring in me, when I met thee, a fine feeling it was!"

Hilda lay her head on the shoulder of James, "Twas a feeling so strong I was hoping thee felt as I did." She lifted her head from his shoulder, and looked into the kindness of his eyes. "I feel it is the same as yours," he said, "I've a kin to ask thee, of thee growing up in the Craggs," said James. "Got to know a fair number of friends o'ert years." James waited for some back chat from Hilda. "There's lots I can fill thee in wi what's in my mind," she said, "That's if thee wants to blab about the Craggs." James was laying in relaxed comfort.

Hilda's words may reveal some interest to James that could bring Katy into the conversation. James had a yen that they had mixed as friends.

James also thought that Hilda knew of the fling he had with Katie. He didn't want to bring too much emphasis, bringing Katy into his intended conversation. He was confident that the rapport they had together was safe enough to open enquiries of his past association with Katie without damaging the trust they were building up between them. The early evening dusk and the quiet atmosphere on the boat was a perfect feeling of tranquillity that set the scene to create an intimacy that they both longed for. "Thy knows of me past with Katie Wainwright, Hilda?" James looked at her and waited for her response. "There were snippets of talk which were banded about. Note much to shout about." Hilda rolled over to James to get some closer comfort to his relaxed pose. "When thee found the body of Sam Lister, gossip passed around the Craggs, but it died away after a while." James pulled Hilda to a more comfortable closeness, "Katie's father, Henry Wainwright, does thee know owt of the way he treated Katie?"

"She was bullied by him," said Hilda, "Her life was controlled to the strictest of limits. She was sheltered and had to obey his code of strictness."

James didn't want his conversation about Katie to muddy the waters of discussion that he was enjoying with Hilda. They were warmly embraced in each other's arms, and there was an amorous feeling that was mounting between them. They both knew that they shared the intimacy that had warmed with their closeness. James and Hilda gave way to the most beautiful feeling of ecstasy, their conversation was abandoned and replaced with the heavenly act of love.

The smell of cooking woke the dishevelled Hilda from her bunk, next morning. James was preparing breakfast. He was humming a cheery tune. His mood made Hilda feel at ease. She had woken to a tranquil calm on the small craft. There was no feeling of guilt from their night of passion. James' mood made her feel comfortable as she watched his half naked, young body busy himself preparing breakfast for her. "Thy looks fresh as a daisy," said James as he taunted Hilda, hiding her modesty behind the covering on the bunk. "It's my choice to keep the mysteries of mine from thee lecherous eyes, James Sanderson."

"Thee didn't hide the sen before," said James, "Thy let thee vanity down freely."

James handed his prepared food to Hilda, she looked admiringly at his fine, young torso as he handed her the food. "Get thee sen fed and watered. The boats are to be sorted out for Freddie. He'll look kindly if we do the respects of his craft." James sat beside Hilda, "There will be a next time, if thy's game?" She kissed his warm lips tenderly, "If the next time is offered," said Hilda, "I'm all yours!" James accepted the offer with a passionate squeeze.

James appeared at the late afternoon to the forge, Rusty was pottering with some bits and pieces. "Thy's still faffing about," said James. Rusty eyeballed his son's friendly chuckle. "Looks as thy's had a fair time, me lad."

"A fine time," said James.

"Freddie sends his respect and thanks thee for the doings of the past, he's a good lad to do for," said Rusty. "Me day is done now lad, lets lock up, me and thee can blagg in't Acorn wi a tankard full of cool nectar."

"That'll do for me," said James. "I'll gi thee some chat as to what's chuffed me up. Mind thee, thy's not having some of the details." James winked at Rusty, "I'll not purge thee for the secrets, move the sen, time waits for no man." They vacated the forge and made tracks to the Acorn Inn.

Rosie and Tilly sat together near the comforting fire. It was a quiet period in the late afternoon. Tilly ran toward Rusty and James as they entered the room. Rusty picked up the bonny lass and swung her around his shoulders. Her greeting gave Rusty a buzz of delight. He had planned with Rosie they would take Tilly into their care. Rusty had made an agreed commitment to Rosie. They would vacate the Acorn Inn and live with Rusty and James.

Rusty had hinted his intentions to James before he gave him the free time. He needed the break from James to finalise details of his intentions to house Rosie.

Tilly and the baby hoped that James would be comfortable with the offered arrangements. Rusty and James spent some quality time at the Acorn discussing the changing circumstances that Rosie, Tilly and the coming child were to move into their new home. "Is thee gonna spit the happenings of what thy's been up to on Freddie's boat?" James looked sheepishly at Rusty. Rosie was having a quiet moment. She joined in the small group that were settled around the comforting fire. "Thy's put me in a spot of knowing what to spout to thee and to what I am not gonna," said James.

"Thee must have been sowing the fruits of enjoyment as youngens do," said Rosie, "Bitta fishing, swimming and horse play as thee does. Tommy and Poppy came in here last night." Rosie looked at James, "Thy's been on thee own wi Hilda!" James looked at Rosie, "Nowt to do wi thee. Look after the own doings." James looked at his tormenting friends, "I'm not spouting no more thy way," said James. "Fill the tankard again," said Rusty. "Charlie Horner wants his coffers filling afor't nights over." Rusty lifted his vessel to Rosie.

James left the inn before Rusty. He had arranged to see Hilda at the Craggs. The night was coming to a close at the Acorn, Charlie Horner had retired and left Rosie to close the premises. She did her usual domestics in the empty room and went to close the Inn door. Rosie pushed at the partly open door which didn't move. A large muddy boot held the door ajar, "We are at the end of the night," shouted Rosie to the wearer of the boot that jammed the door. Rosie pushed again, there was silence outside, "Tek thee foot away and be off wi thee." The door was pushed open against the attempted effort of Rosie.

The site before her was a shock. She gave a restrained squeal of terror. "Would me bonny lass shut me out?" She faced the scowling grimace of Josh Tetley, "Thy's altered thee shape lass, thy's not as I left thee." Rosie had no words of reply, she was in fear at the sight of him.

"I left thee wi-out the change that thy's in now," Rosie put her hands on her pregnant stomach, "Who's the guilty rascal that's sown his seed in thee?" Rosie couldn't find words to answer the raged scowl of Josh. "Thy's been gone out of me life. The absence I thought was forever. Thy's on the run from the crimes. I've done things my way and this is my answer to thee, Josh Tetley," she said clutching at her stomach. "If thy's a mind to alter things as they are, thy'll come unstuck. The law is in my favour, do as thee will to suit thee, Josh Tetley."

Rosie stared at the wide-eyed Josh Tetley, "If thee harms me, thy'll make a thicker rod for the own back!"

"I'm in a fix Rosie, it's my doing. I can't find a way out of me fear of the law, me end will come if I fall foul of them." Rosie responded, "Then leave me in the way I'm in. That's the only way it can be Josh."

Josh Tetley kept his silence and walked into the dark night. Rosie watched his forlorn figure fade away. She closed the door and stood for a while with her eyes closed. She clutched her pregnancy with both hands and a torrent of tears finalised her encounter with Josh Tetley.

The forge at Ivanhoe Mill was having a quiet period. Rusty had been called to Cawston Manor by Gunston Cawston. He left James to do his own thing. The freedom of his day gave him the yen to see Hilda at the Craggs. Emily greeted Rusty at the side entrance hall to the manor.

"Mr Cawston is ready to receive you, Mr Sanderson." Rusty acknowledged her with a smile and nodded with approval. Emily knocked on the door of Gunston's study. The reply from within signalled Emily to open the door for Rusty. He faced the calm looking Gunston who sat relaxed in a chair smoking his pipe. "Ah! Good morning to you, my dear

Rusty." He signalled for Rusty to be seated, "There is much to be discussed today." He extinguished his pipe; the remnants of his tobacco were emptied into a vessel at his side.

"The things we have already discussed, Gunston, have been carefully considered by me. My circumstances with what have been ongoing with Rosie and yourself have opened up a constructive solution to the expected changes that I am having to make."

Gunston Cawston looked wistful at Rusty, "What I am seriously proposing." Gunston arose from his chair and faced Rusty in a calm manner. "The time has come for me and you yourself, know that I have indicated over the years that James has now matured into a time that we have to make a transition for him to start inheriting in a compromised way that we both agree is the right solution for everyone to benefit. At the time of James' birth, there was a serious problem. We both dealt with it in a way that was difficult, my guilt at that traumatic time when James' mother died in childbirth was a moment in my life that turned me from being selfish and taking advantage of your woman that was in my employ, hence the birth of James."

Rusty listened quietly as Gunston spilled his acknowledgement of the past to him. "I have accepted from the birth of James that you have set me up honourably with the forge and all that has come with it," said Rusty. Gunston sat down in his chair, his hands clasped. He looked at the handsome figure of Rusty with an intense look on his face. Gunston rang his bell for attention, Emily answered the call, "Emily, refreshments for Mr Sanderson and myself." Emily acknowledged gracefully and left the study, closing the door gently.

After the welcome refreshments, Gunston and Rusty were set to settle the business plan that Gunston was to propose. Rusty looked at the Lord of the Manor, his elegant stance looked quite superior to the seated Rusty. "At the time, I was in turmoil that what happened at the birth had phased out any understanding of how to deal with it." Rusty faced the stir of Gunston, the memories of the past were vivid in Rusty's mind. "I admit you made good in an honourable way," said Rusty.

"The fact that you gifted me the forge, was a fine thing for you to do." Gunston stood facing the large bay window in his study. "Because I have no kin who can inherit from me, I have given great thought as to how I can put my affairs safely in place."

Gunston turned from the window, looking at the seated Rusty.

"It is all legal and binding," said Gunston. "I have a great number of properties around the village of Ivanhoe Mill, they need settling appropriately."

Rusty stared with anticipation at Gunston, waiting for his words that would explain their being together in these discussions. "I am aware that your circumstances are soon to alter," said Gunston, "I do like to discreetly know of the happenings around Ivanhoe Mill." Gunston looked at Rusty, "Your lady, Rosie, is with child, which is no business of mine, and you have chosen to be benevolent adults of young Tilly." Rusty replied, "I have committed myself to look after their welfare. Why are my affairs being discussed in this manner?" Rusty looked at Gunston for his reply, "The Lister Farm." Rusty looked at Gunston, "The Lister Farm?" said Rusty, "What about the Lister Farm?"

Rusty looked in a puzzled way at Gunston, "That is what I have been leading up to my dear friend, I own the Lister Farm. The two Lister brothers that have been caring for it since that awful tragedy, are to relinquish their tenancy. I have in mind a way that I am hoping would be to your liking and put James on a ladder of inheritance and satisfy my yen for securing his future." Rusty looked at Gunston in awe at his implied suggestion. "Does tha mean for James and I to turn farmer from blacksmith? Is that what thy's saying?" The now smiling Gunston Cawston replied, "Not at all, if it comes to pass that you will take up my offer, it would be to my hoped pleasure you will not be immediately plunged into the unknown territory of becoming from Blacksmith to farmer."

"The transition of you moving from your present occupation would be over a period of time to suit you and James. The Lister brothers will settle your anxieties of running the farm." A knock on the study door was answered by Gunston, Emily entered with refreshments. "Thank you," Emily placed her tray down gingerly between them and left the room with a courteous nod.

After a break in their discussions, Gunston started again to outline his offer. "The accommodation," said Rusty, "How will that be settled?"

"The farm is adequate for you to be in comfort," said Gunston. "Keep the forge and farm workable until the time comes for you to settle on a permanent basis."

Rusty replied, "The most pressing question I must ask, will the farm, be settled lawfully in the name of James?"

Gunston looked at Rusty with sincerity, "The farm has been dealt with, James is securely installed without problem. James must be kept in the dark as to such a time when he will be offered the inherited land and farm. Does that suit your way of thinking, Rusty?"

He looked wistfully at Gunston who gave him a glass of sherry. "I drink to that with you, Mr Cawston. You are an honourable gentleman, I have the greatest respect for your sincerity, Cheers!"

The outcome of the talks between Gunston Cawston and Rusty Sanderson was discussed with James who had a profound interest of the planned transition to move to the Lister Farm. Rusty explained to James that the forge would still be an ongoing place of work for them. The addition of Rosie and Tilly and the expected child would be more beneficial to all. The Lister brothers would gradually integrate the Sanderson's to the workings of the farm and their own choice to hire any needed help. If they required any extra help in the forge. James was quite intrigued with the challenge put before him by Rusty. After his thoughts of being farmer and blacksmith, it gave James exiting thoughts for the future. It also gave him an aspiration of hope. Rusty explained to James that Gunston Cawston had requested Rusty that his success over the years doing a most credible job at the forge made him to offer the Lister farm to them. However, until such time that James could be told that he was the beneficiary in waiting, it would have to be done in the strictest of secrecy and kept from James.

"It's a girl!" said the local midwife at Ivanhoe Mill. She stood at the bedside of Rosie, passing her the child. Rosie had a traumatic birth; she took the new-born from the midwife. Rosie's exhaustion had drained her of the expected pleasure she hoped for. "There now, my brave lady, thy's done the job. They'll see the pleasure of what's been through in a short quickness of time."

Rosie smiled her thanks as the busying midwife settled her to comfort. Rusty entered the room, his beaming smile quelled the hurt of the birth. "Thy's done a fine job, Rosie," said Rusty, "A pleasured day it is! I need to spoil thee and treat thee for giving us such a prize!"

Rusty thanked the midwife and went back to the forge with his glad tidings of joy to tell James and friends he passed on the way.

The weeks after the birth were the time for a transition of arrangement to move into the Lister farm. Rosie had rallied to her usual self, and with Tilly's help they held a fine relationship of sharing all that lay before them. The Sanderson's shared any time they had away from the forge to work with the Lister brothers. James and Rusty were formulating their plans to eventually run the farm to their own requirement. Before Rusty and his new family were eventually ready to move to their newly acquired farm, Tilly experienced a problem that was in her mind of that terrible winter when she lost her parents and younger sister. But careful reassurance from Rusty and Rosie gave Tilly security in her thoughts of the past to accept going back to the farm of the past tragedy. Tilly was still fearful of the past. Rusty and Rosie were desperately looking for a solution to satisfy Tilly's fears. Rosie had given her a caring role looking after the new born baby. They hoped she would settle with her responsible position that Rusty and Rosie had given her. They all eventually settled into their new life at the farm. The Lister brothers were still providing Rusty and his family with their guidance and hard work which was needed before they eventually left the Sanderson's to their acquired property.

"Lola, Lola, you bony little darling. Look what Aunty Tilly has for our sweet baby!" Tilly Lister looked admiringly at Lola, Rusty and Rosie's child. She was seated securely in her high chair, her gleeful expectation of the food that Tilly was preparing to offer was such a delight to see. "Be secure with her, Tilly my love. Don't let her prattle and slop about. Get the victuals inside her belly and not scattered abart!"

Tilly tormented Lola with her filled spoon of food. She made a game with her, tempting the lively child to obey her feeding efforts. "Nearly finished with the little mite, Rosie?" said Tilly, "She wants to be a player, not a feeder today!" Tilly finished her feeding chore and settled Lola in her perambulator. Tilly was quite settled in her routine at the farm. Her chores were constant throughout the long day. She was very adept at her treatment with the farm animals, and her strength of character helped the family unit. Rosie called Tilly her little Gem.

"If thy's a mind to Tilly, James has a trip to the crags to fetch stock for the farm." Tilly acknowledged the words of Rosie, "When thy's ready, the trip to the Crags will give thee a bit of freedom from the chores. Thy's said a good thing to me Rosie, I'll be glad of thee break," said Tilly. She looked at her adopted mother with love and a feeling of security. Her plump figure and ruddy face was all that Tilly needed to feel safe about having Rosie guiding her with her pleasant personality.

The Sanderson household had now a sense of order. Rusty and James had contributed very skilfully to their newly acquired property. The Lister brothers had now left the farm, leaving the Sandersons in a very favourable position. "I'm ready when thy is," shouted James as he waited for Tilly. They were to go to the crags in the horse and cart for supplies that had been delivered and were waiting to be picked up. "Put the thick covering on Tilly," said Rosie, "There is a chilly nip in the air. Don't want thee coming down wi ought that's to tek thee off the feet. Lola needs thee in good fettle." She looked with love at the young, bonny Tilly, "I need thee in a robust state, me lass. My task would be a burden wi out thy help." Tilly took heed of Rosie's mothering and joined the waiting James. They set off to the Craggs, Rosie watched their departure with a friendly wave.

Since the Sandersons had taken residence of the Lister farm, James and Hilda's relationship had been quelled to a minimum. The time spent at the farm and the forge left no time for their courtship to be satisfactorily fulfilled by the wants of Hilda. James spent a large portion of his time with horses.

The farm had acquired a number of animals that Rusty and James had found to be necessary to fill the void at the farm to suit their intended requirements. Gunston had also had a discreet meeting with Rusty, offering his stable facilities to him with the intention of integrating James to take his offered opportunities of horseman ship.

It was part of his plan of inheritance to strengthen his future with his role of working in the domestic atmosphere of the stabling and welfare of the animals. James had been riding around Ivanhoe Mill with cocky confidence for some time since they came into this possession of the animals. He had developed an air of superiority. His altered attitude was scorned at by many of his friends. However, certain friendships were maintained by James. He still pleasured some of his free time with a small number of his friends at Ivanhoe Mill.

James had acquired his horse transport to travel further afield from his routes around Lime Craggs and Ivanhoe Mill. The fruits of his newfound pleasures in the surrounding area had given him the capacity to seek newfound delights. This gave him a fresh insight into his expanding world. It was on a visit to an outlying village some miles from Ivanhoe Mill, that he passed a young couple. They were pushing a large wheeled hand cart. It was heavily loaded with what looked like their belongings. The young lady carried a child, cradled in a sling around her frail body. James stopped a short distance ahead of the couple and waited for them to draw level with him. They stopped, looked up at the fine-looking James who sat proudly on his horse.

"Good day to you," said James looking down at the forlorn sight behind him. "Good day to you, sir," replied the young dishevelled man. He released his grip on the shafts of his hand cart, and looked sadly at James. He had a pleading look on his thin, gaunt face. His silence prevailed as he waited for James to address him. "You look hassled and weary with your load," said James. "We are in a state of distress," said the young man. He looked at the young woman and child, "Is there a place nearby to take water for my horse?" said James. "A short way up yon," said the young man pointing ahead of James. "Your needs may be suited, sir. Just ahead, just ahead."

James rode his horse slowly in the young man's pointed direction. He soon came to a number of rickety buildings set back from the narrow lane. He tethered his horse and walked towards an open-door residence which looked rather public. A few rough tables were displaying vessels of ingredients to use as to when food or drink were purchased on the premises. James sat on a rough bench, and placed his cap and whip on the table before him. "Gooday, sir," a chubby middle-aged bearded man stood at the side of James. "And to you as well," said James with a respected reply. "If thy's got the refreshments of my needs," said James, "That'd be my pleasure."

The chubby man gave a list of what he could offer. James sat contentedly on the bench and waited for his ordered refreshments. As he sat wistfully thinking, he felt thankful that his life had turned to such an exciting venture. His mind was so full of intentions that he wanted fulfilled. The fat gentleman appeared with the order, "For you with respect, young sir," said the fat man. "Tha's served to me pleasure," said James. The beaming face of the fat man left James to enjoy his leisure.

James looked over at the passing family who had directed him to where he was enjoying his refreshment. He beckoned them over to where he sat outside the Inn. The young man released his grip on the cart he was pushing and looked at James. "Come over to me, if thy's a mind too," shouted James. "I've a mind to ask things of thee." The young man looked at his woman and child, "If thy's a wish to hear me words get thee sen over to me." They looked at each other in anticipation of James who had beckoned them to join him. They left their belongings and walked slowly towards James. "There is no cause to be afraid of me," said James, "I like to offer thee somet to put yourself in comfort."

"Drink and eat wi me, it's my pleasure," their shy response was made easy as James used his kind personality. James shouted for the fat man, who immediately appeared with his beaming smile to satisfy the demands of his welcome customer. "Tell the man what thy wants. Don't be afraid of asking. The pleasure is for me to bless thee with." James looked at the young infant who whimpered in the mother's arms, "Ask without any fear of the wants of the young sprog."

James shouted again for the fat man, "Settle the youngen, my friend. She needs what thee can offer to settle the young lassie." The fat man spoke to the mother asking for the baby's needs. She turned nervously to James with her thanks. "The pleasure is mine," said James.

The young family who thankfully accepted the offer of James was shy in their conversation. Since James had seen the sad sight he had witnessed, it had sparked a desire in him to enquire of their obvious distress. The young man looked at James, "Why has thee offered this kindness? We are but strangers to thee." James looked kindly at the family, "My want to help the obvious plight thy is in is the answer to you. I have given thought to what situation thy is in. You look run down to what looks like a bad run of luck!" The young man was in a mind to talk in a way of James. He was thinking it was a way of sharing the bad luck that had befallen them. "We are on the road sir. Our dwelling has been taken from us. We have only the means of wondering and the wish for any kind of shelter. This kindness from you sir is a sign that goodness is around."

James was mindful of thoughts that had filled his mind that the wants of this young family would be satisfied with a break of goodness they prayed for.

"Looking at the way thy's fixed in the here and now, the choice thy has is at its lowest eb. I have thoughts and a way out of the problem to suit thee, if thy has a mind to listen to my offered words." The young man looked pensively at James, "Say what's on thee mind, sir. I would respect what thy's to say!" James had made his mind up what offers he had to make to this family unit from his first sight of them, he had been formulating the struggle they faced. He put himself in their position. What way out would there be if he had faced the same hardship?

James was fixed in his mind; the offer of his thoughts was to ask the young man if he was interested in what he had to say. "I live in Ivanhoe Mill," said James, "Its several miles from here." The young man nodded, "I know of it, sir but never have been there." James explained, "I have a farm and a blacksmiths' forge. My father and family live there. I have recently taken tenancy of the farm, but I have some employment of work. If thy's of a mind to take my offer, it would help me and give thee a boost to live free from thy bad luck." The young couple were overwhelmed by the words from James, "Thy's telling us sir, as strangers that the words you have spoken are your true saying?"

"My offer is as how I have said," said James, "Thy'll be secured and sheltered. I'll get thee to Ivanhoe Mill to settle."

The young man's face came alive with pleasure, he looked at his lassie. She had the same pleasured look on her face. James beckoned the fat man to the table. "I have to ask thee, my friend, for a horse and dray to hire for a trip to Ivanhoe Mill. Can thee supply?" The fat man went back indoors to ask about the request from James. After a short while, he came from within the inn and gave him directions that he wanted. James told the fat man to look after the family's needs until he returned. After an anxious wait, James returned. He tethered his horse and went to the waiting family. "Good news to tell thee," said James, "Horse and dray will be here in a while, then it's off to Ivanhoe Mill."

The man and his woman looked at each other with relieved pleasure, "The goodness of heart thy has shown us, Sir, how can we pay thee for such a blessed kindness?" James looked at the young family, "My reasons are for me to pleasure," said James. "I thank thee for your acceptance of my offer to come back with me to my farm at Ivanhoe Mill."

The horse and dray finally arrived at the Inn. It was soon loaded with the family's belongings. James rewarded the fat man for his kindness. His beaming smile never left his face. "To Ivanhoe mill," said James. They arrived at the farm in the early evening. The last part of their journey was in a downpour of heavy rain. They arrived at the farm. James sheltered them in the barn. "Make thee comforts as best thee can," said James, "I'll come back to thee when I have made my presence known back at the farm house." James stabled his horse and went indoors to speak of his bringing the family back for them to work and settle on the farm.

What James had done had mixed feelings from Rusty and Rosie.

The deed was now done, "The baby they have," said Rosie, "Fetch them indoors from the down pour. They will be in a sorry state." James went to fetch the mother and child from the barn. The two men were happy to settle until the morning. They were soon settled into a routine. James knew they would benefit his plans to expand the farm. Rusty had his workload increased. He and James were now enjoying their additional role in the life of blacksmiths and farmers. The expansion of their gains had given them a new impetus to succeed in their venture.

James had been afforded unwittingly many learnings of the gentry at Cawston Manor. Gunston encouraged him to get conversant with his added privileges at Cawston Manor, he had risen in the eyes of many to a very gentlemanly product of the way he had been groomed. James felt that his transformed newfound role in life made him question why he had risen to such heights of excellence.

Joseph, who was still in the employ at the manor, was talking to a young man about the age of James. They were attending to a horse held by the stranger, Joseph shied off their connection when James came to them. "Now then, Joseph. Is thee still spinning the yarns of make belief thee cursed me with?" The young man who was finally dressed stood upright to James; Joseph stood apart from the confronted pair. "Why might we have the pleasure of such a bumptious cad?" the well-dressed young man said.

"I am James Sanderson, if you please. I am a blacksmith and a farmer in the village of Ivanhoe Mill," said James. His cockiness was levelled at the well-dressed man.

"My oh my, that is a fine title to swank around," he pouted his mean lips in an arrogant gesture to James.

"Thy have the manners and pretence of a man that the arrogance of thee words needs stunting," said James. He looked in defiance at the obnoxious young man.

"Begging your pardon, James," said Joseph stepping forward.

"This is the nephew of Mr Cawston. He has just arrived from the estate of Sebastian Dangerfield. I am to take him inside to his uncle." Joseph looked at James for a reply, "Let's hope his arrogance won't continue in the manor," said James boldly.

"I will take your fine words to my uncle," said the young man. His lispy twist of his gesture nauseated James as they went into the manor. James made his way to the stables to see the groom that looked after his horses. Joseph made haste to his duties at the manor, not wanting a confrontation about his past incompetence to make James and Katie meet. Emily escorted the nephew of Gunston Cawston to the master's quarters. "You are Richard Dangerfield, young Sir," said Emily in her respectful enquiry of the young man.

"I am indeed that person," he said. His sneer had sharp edges which showed his arrogance.

"Your nephew, Sir," said Emily as she ushered him into the study of Gunston Cawston.

Gunston Cawston greeted his nephew with a cool stare. He had been sent for a strict and important interview by his uncle Sebastian Dangerfield to assess his worthiness of being a member of the Estates he was born into. He has let down his beneficiaries to such a degree with his abusing that has been afforded to him. His heavy gambling and many inappropriate blunders have put the estate in a deflated danger of its viability of being liquidated. "You are before me today, Richard, under unpleasant circumstances. I am to assess your worthiness as to whether you are of benefit to remain in our family unit. I know of your misgivings. You know too. The lessons and warnings over this latter period of your life now has to be assessed."

Gunston stared with disgust at his none favourite nephew. "My brother Sebastian is at the end of his tether with the trouble you have caused him. His heath has deteriorated to such a degree that his doctors have put emergency measures in place to keep him in a manageable state of health, and YOU, you are the main contributor to this debacle." Richard with head bowed, was unable to look at his uncle Gunston.

"Look at me as a man," Richard lifted his head, looked at the angry figure of Gunston Cawston. He still had a look of twisted defiance, even a touch of bravado, he had never been in a position of this calibre before. He had always absorbed the blames of his accusers and escaped any real punishment. However, he now felt he was trapped and was at the point of no return. "To save the estate of Sebastian, for him, I will bail him out with the losses you have accrued. You alone have had the knife, at the throat of the Dangerfield Estate, and you alone have caused the depths of depravity and this is the final end of your being connected to the Dangerfield's. I want you out of my sight and out of the lives. Go and earn an honoured crust in the world without ruining everything you selfishly touch. Go now laddy, go laddy, GO."

Gunston Cawston had no choice but to banish his nephew from the estate of his brother Sebastian. It was strong in his mind that it couldn't survive much longer. Bankruptcy was imminent. He knew his last gasp input to save his brothers problems were futile. His health was getting to the point of no return. Katie who had been groomed to her now present position of Lady in waiting to succeed Sebastian on his passing. Katie had been integrated into her position of First Lady with the plotting of Sebastian and Cawston. To make Katie's position lawful at Dangerfield, the exclusion of Sebastian's nephew to claim any inheritance on his estate had been eliminated in Katie's favour.

Back at Ivanhoe Mill, the Lister farm had taken on a more prosperous outlook, expansion and updating of a now named Sanderson Farm had given the whole area of Ivanhoe Mill a richer role that benefited the whole village. James spent much of his time at Cawston Manor. His grooming of Gunston's secret plan that was to be passed to James gave him an impetus to satisfy his dream that the Cawston Estate would be safe in the foreseeable future.

Chapter Eleven
Katie Returns to Cawston Manor

There was much anguish and concern at the Dangerfield Estate. The help from Gunston Cawston to rescue his uncle Sebastian from bankruptcy had not provided the solution to keep the Dangerfield Estate viable. Growing concern of Sebastian's health was now a problem that was affecting the whole household. Katie, who had been caring for her adopted Uncle, now held the reins of power. Getting rid of the treacherous Richard had made her role of managing the affairs of the estate less strenuous. The staff were aware that their employment was in danger. Katie had no answer to their fears of losing what they had. She had visions of her own, wondering what may become of her if the Dangerfield Estate went into liquidation.

Katie had been nursing Sebastian for quite a long period of time. He spoke to Katie when he wanted to share his fears and aspirations of what her future held. When she first came to the Dangerfield Estate, Sebastian's plans for her had already been formulated by Gunston and himself. She had risen with flying colours to her now position of Lady of the Manor. Her future, she thought, was now in doubt. However, Sebastian told her that the future was secure and safe. Katie had questioned him of what he was trying to tell her, but his comments to Katie were left for her to wonder what her future held. In the wake that when the time came for her to move on to something new, she would meet the challenge in her own indomitable way.

The time had arrived when Sebastian Dangerfield's health was now causing serious concern. Word of his failing health, had been sent to Cawston Manor, to his brother Gunston to come to his bedside with urgency. Katie knew that his time was near. She hoped that Gunston Cawston would be in time to see his brother before he passed away. The thought of meeting Gunston, gave Katie mixed feelings of her time spend at the Cawston Manor. She had not seen her father since she had been at the Dangerfield Estate. She hadn't felt any guilt, in fact her mind had quelled at the thoughts of her father. She still had aspirations of James, she often tangled with the thoughts of him with great sadness when thinking of him.

Tears would flow and she always chastised herself when her thoughts of him came to the surface. Katie had been urgently preparing the necessary domestic needs for the arrival of Gunston Cawston. He was expected in a short time at the Dangerfield Estate. Katie had been in constant attention with her staff and doctor. Sebastian's time was near to its end. Katie prayed that brother Gunston would arrive in time. She was at her wit's end with exhaustion and wished that her constant nursing and the ensuing results would soon reach its conclusion.

"Begging your pardon, Miss Katie, Mr Cawston has arrived." Katie acknowledged the maid, "Give him the required assistance and bring him to me in the sick quarters of Mr Dangerfield." The maid nodded respectfully, and went to attend the request from Katie. Gunston was taken to his brother's room by the maid. He knocked gently on the closed door. It was opened by Katie. She smiled and greeted Gunston. She had not seen him since her departure from Cawston Manor. He looked much older now, but still had the kind, assured manner he treated her with, when she worked at Cawston.

Gunston hugged Katie gently, and kissed the top of her head. He held her at arms' length and smiled with pride at the now mature, beautiful Katie that faced him. "You have turned into an angel, my dear girl," said Gunston. Even though Katie was in her exhausted state, he saw the underlying beauty beneath. "It's so good to see you, Sir," said Katie with a tired smile. "Come," Katie ushered him to the bedside of Sebastian. Gunston looked with sadness at the depleted state of his brother. He looked at his doctor who smiled weakly at Gunston. "He nears the end now, Sir," he said to his brother, "I leave you to do your grieving."

The doctor left the room, leaving Katie with Gunston Cawston. "I would like to offer my sincere thanks to you Katie. The way you have given such a long period of time, nursing my brother, has been magnificent." She looked at Gunston with tears in her tired eyes, "I just hope that I have done a deed of comforting that is to your satisfaction." Gunston comforted her with genuine tenderness, "You have been heaven sent, my dear. You have given comfort to us all, with your love and dedication.

Gunston offered Katie a seat in the room, "I will call for the comfort of a refreshment. I would like to talk to you seriously about your future that is my dear, if you are in a receptive mood in these present circumstances." She looked at Gunston, "I would like the company that we share to wait for Sebastian to reach a peaceful end."

"As you wish, Katie," they quietly relaxed in a sombre mood. The maid appeared with refreshments. Gunston and Katie continued their vigil with anticipated observance.

Sebastian passed away peacefully. He never woke up as Gunston patiently waited for his life to expire. However, he was thankful to be at his brother's side at his passing. The arrangements for the funeral had been ongoing for some time in anticipation of his death. The gloomy prospects of the Dangerfield estate had now taken presidency of what would now happen to the staff and the bankruptcy they were all embroiled in. Gunston Cawston had taken the liberty to extend the estates viability that would give it a short stay of execution before its closure. Katie had been requested by Gunston to have a serious discussion about her future. He wanted her to recover to a free state of mind for a while, until they could discuss what he had in mind. Katie nervously anticipated the next direction she would take, and what would become of her.

"Katie, my dear lady, if you have any nervousness about our confrontation, I am nervous too." Gunston looked at Katie, the pride he now saw in the womanly figure before him, had given him the hope of what he was to offer Katie. "Since you have been here Katie, you have excelled all expectations that my brother and I hoped you would. You have matured over the last few years and become the envy of all that you have been in contact with. Now that you will be shortly leaving here, what your thoughts and plans would be to satisfy your next challenge you may want to pursue?" asked Gunston.

"Since your brother Sebastian has been ill, I hadn't had the time as to what lies ahead in my life." She arose from her chair, walked towards the heavily draped window and stared at the scene outside in silence. "There is another challenge out there Katie that I know you could fill with honour," said Gunston. Katie went back to her chair. She sedately sat down and faced the calmness of Gunston Cawston. "What may that be?" asked Katie.

Her manner was sharp and sceptical. "When I made the arrangements for you to come here and work for my uncle, there was an underlying reason that both I and Sebastian thought you would be the answer we needed to fill the legacy of inheritance. We wanted you to fill that void, you have now got the seal of approval that you have earned."

"Come to the point, stop dallying with vagueness, with your mysterious connotations you are trying to explain."

"Don't be vexed in your thoughts Katie." Gunston thought that the time was not the best way forward to talk of her future and wanted to leave their talk for a later time. He looked at the exhausted Katie, "You must excuse my inappropriate timing of me selfishly expecting you to absorb what I am asking of you. I will leave you until a suitable time is more to your convenience." Gunston rose from his chair. Katie excused herself and left Gunston to ponder on his thoughts that he wanted Katie to hear.

Over the next few days, the legal team and creditors that were involved with the bankrupt Dangerfield Estate were in consultation with Gunston. Arrangements were made to put the estate in the hands of legality. Gunston had now agreed with Katie that they would have their confrontation to discuss a future role in life that she might consider to accept. They were both in a relaxed manner in the privacy of the garden. Gunston was in a jovial mood and Katie had cast away the stresses of the past, and looked in a more agile state of mind.

"This to me, my dear Katie," said Gunston as they strolled in the unkempt gardens of the estate, "Is what I would like to ask of you. The experience and all the necessary aspects that you have gained living with my brother Sebastian on his estate, have made you the person I would dearly like for you to come back with me to." Gunston stopped short of saying his final words, "You are going to say," interrupted Katie, "Cawston Manor." Gunston with an anticipated look on his face, looked at the stunned Katie, she couldn't answer. They continued their walk around the garden. Gunston held Katie by the arm. They stood together in silence. An age seemed to pass; Katie looked at Gunston. She couldn't answer to his request to go back to Cawston Manor.

"This has come as a great shock to me," said Katie, "I agree to your request, but to return with you has many problems and sad thoughts," said Katie.

Gunston looked for a sign of her acceptance, "Before I can agree to your request," said Katie, "I have to ask and for you to tell me of certain worries that I had left behind when I came to the Dangerfield estate." Gunston looked assuring at Katie,

"We will have in depth and honest discussions about your fears," said Gunston. "I want you to be sure in your mind that any fears you have, I am sure are unfounded and I know you will be treated with great respect."

"I have not seen my father since I left for here," said Katie, "Even though the circumstances were bitter, I felt that you and my father had engulfed me in a situation of acceptance to suit you both." Katie looked at Gunston for a reply to her expressed comment.

"At the time you agreed to go to the Dangerfield Estate. I thought we had sown some seeds of delight that would suit your great personality." Gunston allowed his explanation to be absorbed by her.

"Are the staff still the same as when I had left?" asked Katie. She looked at Gunston's calm smile, "My dear, dear sweet lady, the happenings of the past at Cawston have been entirely modified in your absence. But it is an honest but, your position will be enviable to all at the big house and I know that you would be received with love and respect."

Katie looked a little unsettled as she cast back her memories of Cawston. "It seems I have little choice of turning my future in any other direction in the way you have explained what you have offered."

"The cherry in the pie, my dear girl is that you will be the Lady of the Manor." Katie looked aghast at Gunston's words, "How can that be?" queried the confused Katie, "I hope what you have said is not joviality to give you humour." Gunston kept his smile, "My dear first lady, I will say it again, my beautiful first lady." Gunston now looked serious, "You have been at the Dangerfield Estate for a specific reason, I don't want you to be vexed by what I have said," said Gunston. "I still suspect your words are a mystery to me," said Katie.

Katie felt she was being tormented, "There is no trickery from my sayings," said Gunston, "Let's leave things in abeyance for a while. A final end to our meeting would be better concluded later. I am not trifling with you Katie. All will be decided by you alone. Take some free time. You may want to refresh and ponder. All will be settled I hope to the delight of all."

The steady downpour of rain cast a morbid mood as the mourners of Sebastian's funeral made their way to the small church on the edge of the Dangerfield Estate. Many of the villagers were absent. The weather had depleted their enthusiasm to mourn with the Dangerfield family. The service was conducted at the small church. Lack of enthusiasm was evident. The vicar of the parish did his best to give a true feeling of family loss to all.

Gunston and Katie went through the motions in their own respectful way. They needed to wind up the proceedings that had surely made this a sad day, one not to be remembered with any relish. After the funeral, many arrangements were to be finalised at Dangerfield Manor. Gunston had arranged for a skeleton staff to carry out domestic duties for a short while until the manor was boarded up to a secure state.

The transition to Cawston Manor would then take place. Katie had some personal requests to finalise with Gunston. He had indicated that he would satisfy Katie regarding a special favour to take back to Cawston, Katie's best friend and her ten-year-old daughter. Katie needed the comfort of her friend; they had been inseparable since meeting at Dangerfield. She thanked Gunston for supporting her request that Bethany and her daughter would accompany Katie back to Cawston Manor.

Katie was enthused to ask Gunston about the happenings at Cawston since she had been at the Dangerfield Estate. She would like to be satisfied that she wouldn't be overwhelmed at appearing at her new post if she had not done her enquiries about the present life at Cawston.

Leaving behind the past memories are what Katie would like to discuss with Gunston. She just wanted a picture in her mind to know that she could handle all she was to face with comfort and confidence.

"I do hope Emily is well," said Katie, "We had a kind of understanding. I felt she gave me confidence that made me feel safe." Gunston looked at Katie who reminisced with a faraway look as she pictured her past. Emily knew how Katie came into the world; she was employed at the manor in a junior post when Katie's mother was working at Cawston. Emily had been warned by Gunston to keep from her mind any improprieties she may hear during her employment. She took heed of Gunston's words but her mind carried her own ideas as she worked at the big house.

"She has been a splendid servant to me over the years," said Gunston, "I look after her welfare and the way she provides the services to me is quite a satisfactory product at the end of the day."

Gunston put his hand on Katie's shoulder, "You will have no problem with Emily, my dear." Gunston gave one of his reassuring smiles to Katie. "You are to be the first lady at Cawston, Emily will be delighted to treat you as such." Again, Gunston gave his look of assurance, "I don't feel phased by Emily," said Katie, "We seem to have a bond of mutual respect. I am looking forward to seeing her again. I do hope she likes my friend and her young daughter."

She looked at Gunston for reassurance, "She will welcome you all with a spirit of joy, Katie There is no fear that awaits you at Cawston," he hugged her gently.

"Let's have a refreshing drink my dear. When you have all your enquiries of fear answered, and you feel that the picture in your mind is satisfied, we will move to a conclusion of taking you back to your roots." Katie looked wistfully at Gunston, "There are just a few more details I would like confirming, I would like to confer a little later, excuse me for now, I need to freshen up, thank you for this wonderful conversation." She looked at Gunston, "You are so kind. I feel quite exhilarated with our forward-looking plans." Katie left the room, leaving Gunston to enjoy his aperitif.

Katie went up to her quarters to reminisce the conversation she just had with Gunston. She had kept a few awkward questions from him until she found it appropriate to enter into her area of concern. Bethany, her trusted and much-loved companion, was helping Katie to pack her belongings for the long journey to Cawston. Bethany had enthused her daughter Lucy with the excitement of a new home and many tit bits of joy which would make her happy. She had accepted her mother's explanation that their new life at Cawston Manor would be beautiful and exciting with a treasure of new things to do.

Bethany felt at ease with her daughter's acceptance of her new home. "My dear, Bethany," said Katie, "The more I think of our move from here, the more excited I become." She looked at her beloved companion, "I was rather scared a while back with wanderings of our uncertain future." Bethany looked at Katie. She cherished her friend so much. She gave such a comforting hug. Tears welled in her eyes, and she smiled thankfully with the thoughts that they were going to a new home and would still be together.

"Thank you for giving me your support," said Bethany, "My excitement has increased now that things will soon be settled here at Dangerfield's." A jovial cry of glee was shouted by Katie, "Cawston here we come!" She smiled broadly, "Call for tea, my dear friend. We surely can afford that small luxury."

"Your demand will be carried out my dear lady," Katie looked with pride at Bethany, "Don't think there's cheek in my words, Katie. I just feel so in tune that I'm to serve you as my special friend." Katie held her lovingly, "Let's have that tea."

The hard work of arranging the transition at Dangerfield's was completed over the next few days. Gunston and Katie talked incessantly about the outstanding fears of hers. She had concern for the state of her father's health. To see him again after such a long period of time gave her a feeling of guilt.

She always had it in her mind that Gunston and her father, Henry had plotted her move to Dangerfield's. Even though the past years had been a most exhilarating and valuable experience and made her status to the level she now holds, she would dearly like to have the luxury of closure and peace of mind. Gunston assured her that Henry Wainwright would be fine. He would genuinely welcome her and praise the lord that they had come together again.

After Gunston's conversation with Katie, the master of Cawston Manor relaxed wistfully, absorbing the queries of Katie. No indication of reference about the welfare of James had been mentioned by Katie. Gunston knew that a friendship of James and Katie had been ongoing at Ivanhoe Mill. It disturbed him that their friendship would interrupt his plan that had been plotted to separate them. Henry Wainwright himself and some input from Rusty Sanderson had manipulated the new post of Katie moving to his uncle's Dangerfield estate. Gunston had to find a way of bringing James into a discussion and of his life changing role that had been awarded to him. He felt that he had to let it be known to Katie the status he now held at Ivanhoe Mill.

James and Rusty along with their new child and Rosie and Tilly made up the family unit that was now in place. The Lister farm was now named the Sanderson's. The fact that James had been integrated in life at the manor over the last few years, was the long-term plan Gunston was pursuing as had been done with Katie at Dangerfield's.

Bringing Katie back to Cawston Manor and seeing James in his role, his activities would surely have an effect on Katie as to why she had been awarded her special treatment at Dangerfield's. To find a similarity with the role of James, that surely would to Gunston be difficult explaining to Katie her being sent away to Dangerfield's. This would surely expose the plans that had been perpetrated by Gunston and Henry Wainwright.

James spent much of his time at the stables. He had the facilities at Cawston to work with his acquired horses. His new life that had been made possible by Gunston was well suited to James. Gunston was so proud of his planned inheritor. It had pleased his appetite to bring his son James into his chosen position at Cawston Manor. He would bring the role that James was pursuing at Ivanhoe Mill, the farm and the stables that were given to James for his horses. He would divert her mind to the family life on the farm that the Sanderson's had taken. He hoped that would be sufficient input for Katie and not to have her unsettled about their friendship of the past.

"We will be ready to depart in a couple of days," said the jovial Gunston. He is delighted that the arrangements of moving back to Cawston were now in place. A new beginning was the hope of Katie that she, her beloved friend and her daughter were ready to pursue. Before they were to travel, Gunston had it clear in his mind and mentioned to Katie the status of James. He felt it would relieve him of any pressure that Katie would encounter when they would surely meet as James was a regular visitor to the Manor. He waited for an appropriate time to ease his mind of unsaid things he was to tell her. "My dear Katie, I would like to satisfy my feelings of changes that now exist at Cawston and Ivanhoe Mill. I know it's no business of mine, that you and James Sanderson were good friends back at Ivanhoe Mill and that inadvertently I was aware that the friendship with you and James was maturing to a stronger relationship. Because you were in my employ, I felt it my duty to feel responsible for you."

You now have the capability to make your mark at Cawston Manor. I am sure that I have done the right thing, and my staff will be delighted to have new blood in the house. You will have no problems. Bethany and her daughter, I know, will be a welcome support to you. I am sure that they will be taken in kindly. I must tell you that James Sanderson has been allotted a farm and surrounding property. It is the

Lister farm. He has successfully updated the farm which now employs a good work force. His father Rusty and his new family, Rosie from the Acorn Inn and her baby daughter Lola live at the farm. I must also say that James has acquired a number of horses, he uses the stables on a regular basis which I have given my blessing."

Katie looked at Gunston with a puzzled look at the Master of Cawston. "Are you saying that I will obviously meet James if he has constant use of the stables? I will surely have contact?" She looked at Gunston. Her thoughts of Cawston Manor have now blotted her feelings. She pondered in disarray at Gunston's revelations, "My! Oh my! Mr Cawston," said Katie, "Life at Ivanhoe Mill has surely been shaken up." She looked at Gunston in anger. "My dear Katie, don't misconstrue the changes back at Cawston, don't paint in your mind any adverse problems that may fill your mind." Katie looked at Gunston again with puzzled anger, "It seems I have to reschedule my thoughts that these new revelations have come to light. I feel I have to renegotiate in my mind the added hurdles you have confronted me with."

Gunston tried to look compassionate at Katie's change of mood. "Your fears are unfounded, my dear Katie. Be assured that the changes at Ivanhoe Mill and Cawston Manor will not dampen your expectations that you will encounter." Katie nodded at Gunston, "I will go ahead with what you have said to me," said Katie, "Please accept my apologies if I have been inconsiderate to you." Katie excused herself and left the company of Gunston, "That's alright my dear, do as you will and thank you for listening to what I have had to say."

James was tormenting Lola as she mish-mashed her breakfast. Rosie, who constantly fussed in her organised running of the family, smiled at the antics of Lola as she played the game of breakfast torment that James was enjoying with her. Rosie had grown fond of James, his interacting with Lola showed his love for her and in her mind that was a bonus to Rosie that made her relationship with James special.

Rusty interrupted the game of torment being played by James and Lola. "This is the time of day, lad," said Rusty to his son, "I have the asking of you to spend a bit of thee time wi things I have to say to thee." James looked at Rusty, "What's on thee mind, has thee got the sen in bother? Let's hear what thy's to say." He called for Rosie to settle the mess they had made of the breakfast feed and went outside with Rusty to listen to what he had to say.

"At the Acorn Inn last night, talk of some happenings at Cawston were banded abart." James looked at Rusty with interest, "Is what thy's heard for my ears a bother to me?" asked James. "All I can tell thee is that Gunston's brother Sebastian Dangerfield is now dead and buried, the Estate has gone to bankruptcy, and there is to be some of the household coming back to Cawston with Gunston in a few days." James looked at Rusty, "I heard bits of rumour about changes at the Manor, nowt to bother my head wi." Rusty looked at James, "I've got me stables sorted and there's no bother with them," said James. "The rumour that spooked me was," Rusty looked James in the eye, "Katie is coming back to live in the manor." James turned from Rusty and looked at the landscape before him, "That's no bother to me," said James. He turned to face Rusty, "It's been over between us a while. I've nowt to bother abart. What's gone is gone," said James, "And don't you forget!"

James stared angrily at Rusty, "Katie's father, the snivelling Henry Wainwright, and the weeks of sneaky meetings at the Manor with Gunston Cawston weaving his web of conceit," he looked accusingly at Rusty. "I think you've done a bit of weaving yoursen!" Rusty looked aghast at the onslaught James had thrown at him.

"James," said Rusty, "Since your birth, I have had to content with many problems of survival. The forge was a godsend that gave us the life line to small comforts that saved us from poverty." James listened to the words of Rusty, "Gunston Cawston gave us the forge. It was a settlement on your birth which I had no choice but to accept. From your birth to now, I have been silent with the true facts of your life. I thought you had worked things out since we had been gifted the farm from Gunston Cawston. We have spoken in depth about your future, the time has come for you to know that Gunston Cawston wants you as an inheritor of the estate. I have protected you and myself knowing that one day your life will unfold favourably to an acceptance that you will understand. You are much loved in many ways and you've been a model asset. I just hope that what's happened to your life, James, has been the right thing from me to you." Rusty looked at James for some sort of forgiveness, the pleading look he gave him looked for an answer. James walked away in silence.

Cawston Manor waited with a mixture of anticipation for the homecoming of Gunston and his entourage of new guests from the Dangerfield Estate. There was much speculation about certain posts at the manor. The safety and continuation of the service personnel held doubts that jobs may be lost when the new input from Dangerfield's arrived. Emily had organised comforts and a welcoming for Gunston and his guests. They were expected at the Manor in time for a high tea. Emily had proudly organised the party. She wanted her efforts to be acknowledged by Mr Cawston. Her standing at the Manor was important to her. She always strived to create her status and endeavoured to maintain the pride of her post at Cawston.

The coach party had reached the gates of the manor, the long-graduated slope to the big house which was flanked by the two parallel rows of beech trees, gave a spectacular view of the manor at the top of the hill. The excited residents waited in anticipation for their arrival. The party alighted from the coaches in the courtyard near the manor entrance, and gave out cries of joy and delight of the greeting. Gunston was relieved at the tumultuous reception. The long, weary journey was now to be blessed with the relaxation that was needed to put his house in order for the benefit of all.

Gunston went into his quarters after giving thanks to everyone, and Emily was left to organise the comforts of the newly arrived company.

Gunston had been awake since early dawn. He was hoping that several aspects of the new beginnings would work to his advantage and settle his mind for the future, and give his estate the continued security he had built over the years. His long-term plan which was now near fruition was in place. How to manage the delicate handling of the situation was his main concern.

James and Katie, his true heirs, were to be asked if they would accept what Gunston was to propose to them. It was such a delicate situation. He needed courage and tact to execute the deed of them accepting the offered inheritance. The morning passed slowly, activity at the manor was the start of a new day. Emily had served Gunston with breakfast in his private study. The daily events were to be administered at his request and Cawston would be settled in its routine.

Gunston looked toward the stables from the confines of his study. James was standing beside his horse holding the rein. Katie stood facing James, they looked in silence at each other. The only thought in the mind of Gunston was that providence must be allowed to prevail. The path they choose would be their choice.